A FOREIGN EVIL

DIABLO SNUFF BOOK 1

CARVER PIKE

AUTHOR'S NOTE AND THANK YOU

I've been a fan of horror stories and scary movies since I was a kid. I remember sitting in front of the TV, just a foot or two away from the screen, watching *The Texas Chainsaw Massacre, Poltergeist, The Exorcist,* and *Friday the 13th*. One of the first books I thoroughly enjoyed was *Halloween*, the novel by Curtis Richards that was based on the John Carpenter movie. I've always been fascinated by fear.

This book, *Diablo Snuff: A Foreign Evil*, is my first of what I hope will be many horror novels and novellas.

This book is kind of sick and twisted. I'm warning you ahead of time.

There's a lot of evil out there in the world right now. Just watch the news or read some of the nasty shit that is posted on social media.

But for all that evil surrounding us, there's still a helluva lot of good too.

So I raise this tumbler of Southern Comfort and make a toast to all of you who can still separate fiction from reality, imagination from actuality, and good from evil.

Live out your dark desires through a good book or a movie. Don't do that shit for real.

I hope you enjoy this book.

Before we dive into it, I just want to give a special thanks to the three very special women who read through the newest version of this book to make sure it was clean and ready to put into your hands. Thank you to Mary H., Stephanie A., and Kaye B. for all you do.

1

Let me tell you about the night I experienced true evil. Nothing's been the same since. Mundane things like jogging through the park, watching Saturday afternoon matinees, and meeting Internet hookups at coffee shops seem to have no place in the world once you've experienced the truly sinister circle of life synchronized by Satan himself.

Did I meet the devil? No, but he couldn't have been far away. His presence was painted on the night, slathered on a cosmopolitan canvas of corrupt con artists, sashaying hookers, and pissed-off taxi drivers pressing palms against their horns at every woman they passed and every vehicle that blocked their paths.

I was in a country that was predominantly Catholic, yet, when church was out, many of the citizens over the age of seventeen and under sixty swapped their prayer books, khaki pants, and plaid shirts for the darker threads only seen downtown in the bars and nightclubs.

The devil was there all right. His finger was on the city's pulse, that much was sure. The alleyways and shadowy streets were black lava-filled veins flowing past me down a concrete river as I sat and watched neon signs from strip clubs, sex shops, and casinos reflecting off the damp sidewalks. Rain was constant this time of year. It was a shitty season for a bachelor party vacation. I'd disappeared from my group of friends as soon as I could, which was as soon as the weather let up.

I didn't want to be a drag, but I could no longer handle the constant sensory overload. From the dings and bells of slot machines to the music played live on stage or recycled over ceiling-mounted speakers, the sounds never stopped. My friends could drink whiskey all night, wake up, and then kill their hangovers with mimosas and fried food. They were like bachelor robots only needing to be plugged in for an hour or two each night to recharge and get back to the party.

If my buddies were speedsters zipping around a toy racetrack, I was that one car that always flew off when you pushed it too hard. I moved at a slower pace. My life back home wasn't so extraordinary, and to be honest, I simply couldn't hang. I needed a moment of silence. I found it across the street from the casino.

In truth, my story started with a gaze. *She* was eye fucking the shit out of me.

My mind was on the plate in front of me. Not on the burger itself but on the empty space next to it. I was missing fries, and as I double-checked the Spanish-language menu, I realized the fault was mine. I hadn't ordered any and there were no automatic combos at this restaurant. This place served soda out of cans to ensure you'd pay for a refill and side dishes came at an extra cost.

Shit. Do I order fries now and wait? Or say fuck it and eat the damn burger by itself?

Greasy fries sounded damn good, and I was about to call the waiter over to my table when I glanced up and saw her. Two tables away sat a voluptuous and clearly brazen prostitute. How did I know she was a hooker? She was a single woman out late at night unafraid to look at a man the way she was looking at me now, and she drank soda from a straw while giving it little licks. Regular women didn't drink like that. Regular women didn't look at me like that.

Sex worker, Michael. They're called sex workers now. Have some respect.

Panama City's nightlife was swarming with them, especially in the casino district. I'd learned this lesson the hard way my first night in town when a gorgeous blonde from Colombia approached while I was playing blackjack. The moment I gave her a second glance, it was like I'd claimed her as my own. She clung to my side most of the night and even reached under the table to give my cock a squeeze once or twice. The idiot side of me believed she was really into me and remained that naïve until I noticed the guy watching us from one of the nearby restaurant tables.

"Boyfriend of yours?" I asked.

"No," she replied in a thick accent. "He is Manuel."

"Why is he looking at us like that?"

"Is looking at me. We must go soon or will not be good for me."

"What do you mean?"

Then it hit me. She had the best tits money could buy, wore a dress that was so tight it would need to be peeled from her body, and she was into me. That last part shouldn't have been so strange. I'd never had a hard time picking up women in the past, but this was ridiculous. She hadn't left my side and had been laying the flirting on thick. So thick I felt like a fucking idiot once I realized she wasn't some local who'd found me attractive. She was a high-priced sex worker.

"Please," the girl had said. "Make easy for me. Manuel be angry if I have only one customer tonight. He say is bad for business."

Of course, I didn't want things to be difficult for her. My friends had let out a cheer as I made my way toward the elevator with this beautiful woman on my arm. The sex was unbelievable. I'd never slept with a sex worker before, but in many ways, I figured it wasn't much different from meeting a girl on one of the dating apps.

Modern dating consisted of meeting someplace for the first time, buying drinks, dinner, and whatever else the date called for. Then, if you were lucky, you'd get laid in the end. How was this any different? This time, I hadn't bought drinks or dinner. I was only paying for the sex part, and damn it was good. But it was only sex. That was all.

This girl sitting across from me at the outside patio area of the burger joint did something to me though. I was pretty damn sure she was a sex worker, but it was something about her eyes and her lips and the way she held her straw between her thumb and index finger each time she sipped from her drink. It was like she'd thrown herself across the place and delivered a swift kick to my gut. By that, I mean she damn near knocked the wind out of me.

I was in Panama City, Panama, for my buddy's bachelor party getaway. That's how rich kids roll. They don't do nights. They do getaways. This one lasted four days. My bachelor party, which was for a marriage well-passed over by the time I made this journey, was nothing more than a group of guys hanging out in a strip club and then banging back shots of tequila until a few of us passed out on Fort Lauderdale beach.

Cops don't like people who do that.

This bachelor getaway was beyond my wildest dreams, and I was exhausted. This was our last night in town, and we'd decided to hit the casino area once more. Gary, the groom, had a problem with the dice. It was one of the many vices his wife-to-be would find out about soon enough. This guy could stay at a casino all fucking night if nobody pulled him away. He had the money to burn, so he often did stick around much longer than he should have before finally retiring upstairs with whatever whore he had strapped to his arm. When I left him he was still at the table.

My other two buddies, Coleman and Pete, had disappeared at some point in the night, probably with the two prostitutes we'd had sitting at our table half the night. The girls in the casino weren't shy, that was for sure. Being a single male in a decent suit made you the target of catcalls, kissing noises, and whistles that could rival that of any construction crew trying to get a lady's attention. I'd even had one chick pinch my ass as I walked by.

The regular Panamanian women weren't like this at all. They were very respectful and sweet, or at least the few I'd met while making my way through town seemed that way. These sex workers were ballsy though. They had nothing to lose and everything to gain. This made them brave.

Like this one watching me from her table as I nursed my beer. Once I finally got the waiter's attention, I pointed at the menu and said, "French fries, *por favor.*"

Por favor was one of only a handful of phrases I'd picked up.

"*Papas o patacones?*" the waiter asked. I wasn't sure exactly what he was saying but the inflection in his voice told me he was asking a question, so I pointed at the menu, at the picture of the French fries on a plate next to a cheeseburger, the same cheeseburger I'd ordered, and said, "This. Can I have this?"

"Papas," he replied, nodded, and walked away.

"Papas," I said to myself, trying the word on for size. "Papas."

I was already feeling a bit tipsy and this Panamanian beer was strong. Not strong like it would knock me on my ass but strong like the flavor was acidy. I needed those fries to help stuff my stomach and provide a protective layer.

"*Hey, hermano!*" I heard from the street curb a few feet away.

It was obvious it was directed at me, so I turned toward the man and saw a bald, light-skinned Latino with sunglasses pushed up onto his head. He wore jeans and a white wifebeater tank top. A black button-up shirt was thrown over one shoulder. His attire made me realize he was half-fancy all the time. He went with the flow, drifted up and down the city streets with that tank top on, and if he needed to transform quickly, he threw on that black shirt of his and walked into the ritzier joints.

The taxi he leaned against had to be his because I'd already seen how serious these drivers were about their cars. Many of them had stickers on the back with one stick figure beating another with a club. It had some kind of text that I was pretty sure said, "Don't touch my taxi."

"Me?" I asked, quietly. Really, I think I only mouthed it while pointing a finger at my own chest.

The man nodded. "You wanna go to a club? You drink alllllll night. Get hot pussy. Great time my friend. Hot pussy. I take you there."

I laughed. Pussy seemed to be on offer everywhere in the casino area. The gay scene was very much alive. I'd seen men holding hands and women arm in arm. But I'd yet to be offered some tight ass. Pussy was thrown at me left and right.

How do they know I'm not gay?

Something told me if I asked the guy, he'd know exactly where to take me for some "hot ass." The guy had me pegged exactly right though. I was into pussy. But tonight, I really wanted to just drink my beer, get my order of fries, and eat this delicious looking cheeseburger on my plate. The damn thing had probably cooled down already.

I had a bad habit of letting my food get cold. It was one of the things Adrianna used to bitch at me about. She said I never ate her food when it was still warm. It drove her nuts. Sometimes I missed my ex. She wasn't a bad person. We'd had a decent relationship, up to the point when she cheated on me. For some reason, she thought a hand job wasn't cheating, but in my book it absolutely was.

Her argument at the time? "He didn't even come."

Like ejaculation was the deciding factor.

My response? "That's like me stealing a car and saying, 'but officer, I didn't even make it all the way home.'"

We didn't see things eye to eye. In the end, she moved in with the dickhead whose dick... *head* she'd been so preoccupied with.

"Come on, *hermano*," the taxi driver tried once more. "You pay little, you get a lot. Lot of drink and lot of hot pussy."

"No, I'm okay," I replied. "Thank you for the offer though. Maybe some other time."

The taxi driver shooed me away with an aggravated hand. He mumbled something about gringos and then turned his attention to a teenager who'd touched his taxi. It was clear he wasn't happy about it, even if I didn't speak the language well enough to understand what he said. The teenager ran. I laughed.

I wondered how much commission the driver got for dropping a foreigner off at one of these strip clubs or whorehouses. It must have been a decent sum if he'd decided to park his cab and spend the night trying to convince people to come with him to a club rather than doing his routine driving gig.

Another very hot sex worker passed me and joined the one who'd been eyeing me from afar. My eyes were momentarily glued to them. One was blonde, the other brunette, and both had bright red lips and big fake tits. They were stunning, and I wondered if they liked what they did for a living. Was this by choice or were they being forced into this lifestyle? Were they paying off a debt of some sort or were they lining their pockets?

I'd once had a stripper tell me she made over a thousand dollars a night and she loved her job. She wasn't doing it to pay student loans. Her kids needed things, their daddy wasn't around anymore, and she made a shit ton more money dancing than she ever could in most other jobs. While her friends hustled to sell homes in the real estate game, she shook her ass and made enough money to feel good about herself. I wondered if these two women sitting across from me were happy with their chosen trade.

The first hooker, who by that time I'd nicknamed Salma, pointed at me and both girls giggled. Not like they'd heard the funniest joke ever but that kind of chuckle you give when you want someone to notice you're chuckling. It was the equivalent of high school girls gathering together in a gaggle of their closest friends to call the attention of their cute crush.

I was contemplating whether or not I still wanted to keep the night super chill by finishing my food and fleeing back to the comfort of my room or entice one of these ladies to go with me, when I heard a sweet voice from behind me say, "*Cuidado.*"

Her voice was sexy, with that sultry, smoky kind of rasp only certain women could pull off. I turned around and came face to face with the gorgeous brunette seated behind me. She was alone, and she was different from the other two. She had long hair, just like the others. She had brown eyes, just like the others. She had amazing tits, just like the others. But this girl looked more... real. She didn't give off the hooker vibe the other two did. She had on a tight black dress, kind of like the other two, but she wore a white mini sweater over her shoulders.

"I'm sorry," I said. "Were you talking to me?"

She sipped from a strawberry shake while she plopped ketchup onto her burger from one of the old Heinz glass bottles. The fact that she'd gotten some of the condiment out of its container told me she possessed quite a bit of patience.

Those fucking things take forever.

Glancing up at me while putting the cap back on the ketchup, she fluttered her eyelashes in a playful manner and smiled. I cocked my head to the side and tried to get a good read on her. She didn't know me well enough to be so silly, but there was an instant comfort with this girl. Her eyes glowed ever so slightly, a wonderful sparkle that must have been one of the nearby casino signs reflecting off her pupils.

I was entranced. God, she was stunning.

"You should be careful," she said with the most adorable accent ever. "I tink they like you."

I was so tempted to repeat her version of think but decided against it. Insulting girls, or negging, worked on American girls—sometimes —if done in the right joking kind of manner but it might not go over well here. I'd kick my own ass if I scared this one away or pissed her off enough to make her leave. I was already invested in this relationship even though none had even started.

"Should I go talk to them?" I asked.

"If you want to spend a lot of money to be with a very experienced woman, then sure. Do it. It will be fun."

"You sound like their pimp."

She tilted her head to the side. She didn't understand my joke.

"Never mind," I said. "I don't really want to spend a lot of money or be with a woman *that* experienced."

She smiled. "That's unusual for a... gringo."

"But not men from Panama?"

"Oh, men from Panama are worse. But they go for the lower-priced whores."

We both laughed.

"Where are you from? Colombia?" I hadn't meant the question to be an insult, but it seemed it was. She looked taken aback. "I'm sorry," I quickly tried to recover, realizing I might have already pissed her off. "I didn't mean to insinuate. Are you from Panama?"

"This is my country," she replied.

"Sorry."

"You did not know. That is okay. Do you have experience with the Colombian women?"

"Experience? I don't know if I'd call it that."

"Sex is sex?" she replied questioningly.

She was setting a trap for me. I could feel it. This was the moment where I'd either snag her and keep her here a little longer, or she'd take her food to go and disappear forever.

"No," I replied, "but I've made mistakes."

"Haven't we all?"

Her answer was better than I'd hoped for. Yet, it left me wondering what kinds of mistakes this girl could have made. Was she a prostitute? I'd already fallen for the "girlfriend for a night" routine once before. Was this something similar? Or, had I actually stumbled upon a genuine and beautiful woman who happened to be hungry and stopped for a burger?

I turned my seat so I could see her better, not quite joining her at her table, but definitely not seated with my back to her. She was the most beautiful person I'd ever seen in my entire life, and that was no exaggeration. If I'd made a wish to be sent an angel without wings, this would be it. Heaven couldn't have her back, not without fighting me for her first.

Now that I'd turned toward her, I caught my first glimpse of her tattoos. The wing and head of what appeared to be a mockingbird peeked out from her top, right above her right breast. On the other, I saw what looked like ivy curling out. Her sweater didn't make much more of her visible, and I despised that piece of fabric for robbing me the chance to see more of her.

She wasn't as innocent as I thought if she had that kind of ink. I wondered how much more she had. Conversation turned to tattoos for a beat, then on to work and other trivial aspects of life. Before long, I'd abandoned my table altogether and made my way to hers. Sitting across from her, I found myself so entranced by her eyes that I kept forgetting to blink until my eyes were dry and hurt. Then, and only then, I'd close them for a millisecond too long, only to moisten them and bring her back into clearer view.

The burger was good. The fries were tasty. The beer was working its magic. The view was the best part of the date. It seemed to have become exactly that. A date. We hit it off right away. Her accent drove me crazy and from what she told me, she liked mine too. I didn't know I had an accent, but if she said I had one, then I had one.

She asked my name and I told her the truth. For some reason, when traveling, I'd always lied and said my name was Paul. My military background taught me it was always safer to keep some secrets. Paul seemed like a decent enough name. It was a good neighborly name.

Honey, who borrowed our barbecue grill? Paul.

Who's out there playing 80s jams while working on his car? Paul.

Who's fucking his wife so hard she's screaming out his name? Paul.

When I traveled, I was that son of a bitch. I was Paul.

With her, the truth came out naturally. I didn't need to pretend to be something I wasn't. I didn't have to pretend to be some hedge fund manager or a plastic surgeon or a high-powered mob lawyer. With her, I could be me. So, I told her my real name. Michael.

"I like that name," she said. "It's like the archangel. The one who will lead God's army against the forces of evil."

Oh, no. Here we go. Is she one of these religious nutcases?

I had nothing against organized religion, I just didn't like it crammed down my throat, which was what so often happened. I wasn't in the mood for a war of wits, for a struggle of spirituality, for a fight about faith.

"You look like a Michael," she added.

Her name was Isabelle and she worked at one of the smaller casinos. She'd just gotten off work and didn't feel like going home. She lived with two of her friends and hated how they sat around the apartment smoking pot all the time with their boyfriends. She usually delayed her return home on the weekends. It was better that way. By the time she went to the apartment, everyone was usually passed out.

Secretly, I hoped her friends smoked pot all night long, so she'd have a reason to stay with me.

After dinner, I paid for both meals, we stood up to do that awkward dance where we both looked at each other for an intense full minute, both trying to decide what the next move should be. She couldn't invite me back to her place without the risk of sounding like a slut. I understood that. Yet, I was in the same predicament. As much as I wanted to bring her back to my room, I was afraid that even mentioning it would make her feel like a prostitute.

Come to think of it, I wasn't a hundred percent sure she wasn't one. We hadn't had *that* conversation. What if she was one? If that were the case, I would be so bummed. This girl was different. The thought of sharing her with a hundred other men scared the shit out of me. Even though I knew I'd be returning home to the United States soon, I felt an attachment to this woman. At least for now, she was mine.

"Um," she said.

"Yeah," I replied.

Our awkward moment seemed to stretch on forever.

"Do you like to dance?" she asked.

"Sure," I lied.

A relationship built on lies is a horrible idea. It never works, but the truth was, she could have asked me if I liked cyanide Kool-Aid and I probably would have said yes. I only wanted this moment with her to last longer. For the first time in probably my entire life, I wasn't thinking beyond right now.

This was impulsive. It was unsafe. But I didn't care.

"I used to work at a place," she said at a low volume. "It's a bar. Nothing special, but we can go there if you want."

"I'd like that."

She wasn't kidding when she said it was nothing special. She took me to this seedy little bar at the bottom of some steps beneath a bank building. It was a lot like the location where the dad found Gizmo in the first *Gremlins* movie. A hidden away dive. It was a dark and smoky spot, but it was perfect for the two of us. We didn't know each other well enough and the shadows of the shady place were perfect for enhancing our unplanned night together.

That layer of fog fused with the drinks I was throwing back took me to a whole new plane where it was only Isabelle and me. We danced in that make-believe mist. I moved like a drunken moron, doing the gringo sway, rocking my hips from side to side to salsa and merengue music. When a reggaeton song came on, we practically dry-fucked on the dancefloor.

She seemed to be digging me. It was great. The two of us mingled with other patrons and mixed in among the other couples on the dance-floor. We'd known each other for such a short time, but to everyone around us, we were a couple very much in love.

The way she pressed her body against me whenever a sensual song came on drove me crazy. She held me tight, pressed her tits firmly against my chest, put her face against mine, and moved me to the rhythm of the music. I wasn't a good dancer, but she worked with what she had, and man did she work it.

My cock hardened during the first dance and stayed that way during many of the others. She felt it too. I could tell because of the way she put pressure on me, backing into me and grinding that tight ass of hers against me.

We'd been drinking beer and occasionally throwing back shots of tequila. I was buzzing so good and enjoying my time with Isabelle. It was probably the best night of my life.

During our last dance together, she turned her back to me and shoved her ass against my cock. Reaching for her hips, I moved sensu-ally along to the music, making sure she knew how badly I wanted her. Suddenly, she leapt away from me. Then she drunkenly sashayed back to me and stumbled, wrapping her arms around my neck as she fell into my arms.

"You've had a lot to drink," I said.

"I felt you," she said.

"You felt me?"

"You are very aroused. You like me?"

Do I like you? Are you fucking kidding me? I'm enamored.

"Oh, God. Yes, I like you. Very much."

"You do?"

"You are absolutely the most beautiful woman I've ever seen, and your personality is amazing. You're... you're like perfect."

My words sucked, but I was half drunk, had maintained an erection for hours, and just wanted to fuck this woman. Don't get me wrong, a relationship would've been fine too, preferred, really, as I'd been single far too long, but I wanted to fuck her, plain and simple.

"Ha, perfect? No!" she squealed. "I am not at all."

She was really drunk and the way she spoke drove me nuts. Her accent was thick, and that was sexy enough as it was, but the way she tried so hard to say each word with such grammatical precision, puttering along through her sentences with short pauses between words, made her so damn adorable.

"Yes, you're perfect," I said.

"You want to know a secret?" she asked as she leaned in close to my ear. "I like you too."

Then I felt it. Her tongue, so wet and soft, licked my ear. She took my earlobe in her mouth and bit on it gently.

"Please don't leave me tonight," she whispered. "Take me somewhere. Be with me."

I turned her face toward mine and kissed her. God, her lips were so soft, and to this day, I've never felt a tongue so succulent. I wanted to eat her mouth, to be there in its embrace forever. She tasted so good and we fell into a rhythm that seemed to go along with the music. I grabbed the back of her head and pulled her into me harder.

When she moaned into my mouth I almost came. My cock was pressed so hard against my zipper that I almost lost it. I needed to control myself so if I did get her alone, I wouldn't ruin it with a premature ejacabarrassment.

I took her hand and pulled her toward the door, barely stopping to pay my tab.

"You are excited," she said.

"You have no idea."

Whatever she wanted; I'd be down for it. As I led her up the stairs, her body hugged tightly to mine, I couldn't decide where I wanted to take her. I couldn't take her back to my room because I was pretty sure the guy I was sharing it with, Pete, was already there with one of the hookers from the casino.

I had some cash on me and a credit card, but the truth is I couldn't afford to book a whole new hotel room, at least not at the Sheraton where we were staying. There had to be cheaper hotels around.

When we made it up to the street level, I decided to be honest with her.

"Look, I don't know where to take you. My roommate is busy in my room right now. You know this city better than I do. Where can we go?"

It was lame. I knew it, but I was in a foreign country, on limited funds, with a smoking hot Latina on my arm. What else was there to do? This was her country, so she'd have to know someplace to go. It turned out, she did.

"It's okay. I know. Just take me to a push," she suggested.

"A push?" I asked, wondering what that was.

A strip club maybe? A push?

I had no idea what she was talking about.

"A *push button*," she said as she stuck her hand out to hail a cab. "You have cash, no?"

"Some, yeah."

"Good."

She looked into my face and the lights from the bar and the bank behind me caught her eyes, giving them a neon pink and then green glow, flickering one by one. Her smile was warm, and I couldn't believe how strongly I was already feeling about this girl. It was impossible. No one had ever affected me like this. Not this quickly anyway.

"We can go there then," she added. "There is a *push button* close to my house. I will show you."

2

I'd been to several countries in my life and all of them had one thing in common. It never took long for a beautiful woman to catch a cab. Panama was no different. The second Isabelle put out her hand and waved, the next set of headlights came to a screeching halt. Behind and to the side of this cab, two other yellow taxis honked, obviously upset that he'd won this round.

Isabelle spoke Spanish to the driver and told him our destination. He waved us in and chuckled under his breath. He probably saw this sort of thing quite often. Foreigners whisking beautiful women from his country off to romance them.

When Isabelle snuggled up close to me in the back of the cab and snaked her arm through mine to hold my hand, I noticed the driver watching us through the rearview mirror. I gave him a warning glance and he shifted his eyes to the windshield.

I wasn't going to let him ruin my time with Isabelle. I was in heaven. I'd never believed in the bullshit insta-love stories from all those reality shows, where people go out for the first time, have a few drinks, tell some sob stories, and then make out on the way home only to become an inseparable couple the very next day. Yet, I was experiencing it here in Panama.

The warmth of her body, the hope in her eyes, and the strength at which she gripped my hand like she wanted me to never let go, told me this was something that could quite possibly be real.

And if she's tricking you? If she's a prostitute and this is all a big game to her? Why is that fucking taxi driver looking at you again?

A million thoughts ran through my mind, but Isabelle shut them down the moment she leaned over and pressed her lips to mine. She pulled back only long enough to rest a hand against my left cheek and peer into my eyes for a second. With no words, she warned me not to take advantage of her. She knew I didn't live here and wasn't going to be able to stay, but right now she only wanted to know that I wasn't using her.

This girl wasn't a prostitute. She was a good woman and she wanted to be treated like one. Grabbing the back of her head, I pulled her face closer to mine and slid my tongue through her lips. Unlike me, she didn't care what the driver thought. A soft whimper escaped her and then we were making out like horny teenagers.

"Be my man tonight," she whispered through breathy sighs.

Again, with the secret code shit. What is all this "stay with me" and "be my man tonight?" What does that mean? She knows you can't stay.

I wasn't naïve. I was pretty sure what it meant, but I was a little worried that maybe she was too wholesome to fuck on the first date. What if she was simply drunk and I was taking that for super horny? Maybe she only wanted to cuddle and fall asleep together.

"You want me?" I asked, hoping to draw the words out of her.

"Yes," she said. "I haven't had sex in a long time. I need you."

And there it is.

Like I'd walked into the grand opening at my favorite store, invisible balloons dropped from the ceiling. I was the luckiest man in the country. I'd just picked up the prize of Panama. I'd won the jackpot.

And if her words weren't enough, her hand was totally supporting her answer as her fingers found the zipper to my slacks, slid it down, and reached inside. Her hand was warm as it found my cock and gripped it, her soft touch tickling a little as her fingernails gently scraped me.

"You are ready," she teased.

"Yes, I'm definitely ready."

She giggled. Her attitude had changed so much from when I first met her at the restaurant. A few hours ago, she seemed almost too fresh and innocent. I mean, she did work in a casino so I should have supposed she wasn't a total prude, but this freer side of Isabelle was amazing. She'd let her guard down with me.

I was so into her mouth and the stroking of her hand along my cock that I barely noticed how dark it had gotten inside the cab. I found time to pull away from her tongue long enough to glance out the window.

We'd left the bright lights of the casino district behind. To where we'd traveled, I had no idea. It was a darker area with small supermarkets and other stores that had closed earlier in the evening and now had metal gates covering the doors and windows.

A few people walked the crumbled sidewalks. Stray dogs roamed in a pack, looking so skinny their ribs could be seen through thinning fur. Three old men sat on plastic beer crates outside a tiny house that shared its space with what looked like a barbershop. The business side was closed, but these men weren't ready to call it a night. They sat sipping from cans of the local stuff while listening to tunes on an old radio.

We drove through the part of Panama tourists rarely got to see. This was where the government refused to spend money. Garbage littered the streets and the small houses were painted in odd, unmatching colors. Where the downtown area was mostly high-rise buildings made of glass, this place was all concrete and tin roofs.

I supposed it was why people came to the casino district in the first place. They wanted to get away from the harsh realities of life and spend their weekend evenings pretending every day was the dazzling delights of the metropolitan, where people didn't starve, everyone was happy, and the party never stopped.

We passed a lit-up sign that read: *Amor Real.*

"There's a hotel, let's just go there," I said.

Isabelle laughed. "That's not a hotel. That's a *push button*."

"I still don't know the difference, but if we're going to a *push button,* why not go to that one?"

"You'll see. This one is special. Now pay attention to me, please. I am your woman."

It was a lesson learned. Nothing in the whole world was supposed to matter right now. She was telling me she was right in front of me, giving herself to me, and I needn't concern myself with the landscape or the people on the street or the lights or even the taxi driver watching us once again through the mirror.

Isabelle didn't seem to be bothered about him at all. She looked at him, rolled her eyes, and then reached for the back of my head and pulled me closer. Her tongue once again found mine. But this time she took my hand and slid it under her dress, where she curled my fingers and pressed me against her, giving my hand the okay to scoop up her pussy in my palm.

Fucking hell. Yeah, I'm definitely ready.

I pressed my fingers into the crease between her legs, where I felt the fabric of her panties dampen as they went up inside her. She was soaked. I swirled my finger around her wet pussy, never going beneath the cotton barrier. I wanted her to be crazy for me by the time we reached our destination. She needed to want me as much as I wanted her.

Isabelle moaned and I pushed a little harder, threatening to shove my finger through her panties and up into her. My thumb drifted along the edge of the elastic and felt trimmed pubic hair, not much more than stubble. I loved it.

I wanted to take it in my mouth, to eat her, to make her scream and beg for more.

Fuck, I'm hard. Can this guy drive any motherfuckin' faster?

Isabelle's hips rolled and she tried to fuck my hand, to press herself against my fingers. If this cab driver didn't hurry up and get us there, I was going to yank off her panties and take her right in the back of his taxi. I'd never been so worked up in my life. I'd been married before, and never in that entire relationship had I ever been this turned on. Every part of me felt alive and sensitive, like being near her turned my entire body into a sexual organ.

Finally, the driver pulled over. He said something in Spanish.

"Five dollars," Isabelle said. "Should be three but he's giving us the gringo price. Just pay him so he doesn't bother us."

Bother us?

I imagined him peeking in the window as I fucked Isabelle, softly rapping on the window to "bother us" for the two dollars I owed him.

"Gringo price," I repeated as I pulled out a five-dollar bill and handed it to him.

Where I came from, five dollars wouldn't have gotten us down the block, so it seemed fair to me. In Panama, there were no meters so there was none of that price gouging where the meter started at five bucks. This trip would have cost over twenty back home.

As soon as we stepped out of the taxi, the driver drove off, honking twice as it departed. His horn cut through the night air, making me flinch. The taxi's tires kicked up rocks and disappeared in a cloud of roadside dust, taking with it all the world's sound.

All was quiet.

Too quiet.

Isabelle didn't speak at first, which only intensified the silence.

Without her hand in mine, I was left standing there feeling all alone. Everything seemed bathed in a bluish haze, almost as if the time were only barely beyond dusk, but then I realized it was the light of the moon and a faint glow radiating from the elevated train tracks above my head.

For being a third-world country, this place had a strange modernity. It was a place where the traditional *diablo rojos,* which were old school buses painted with wild graffiti and decorated with bizarre lights, were still used for public transportation. One would also see modern city buses equal to those that roamed the Chicago and Manhattan streets. Plus, elevated trains that dipped into the earth to become subways were a new mode of transportation.

Here, where I stood, the train tracks ran overhead but were lifeless at this hour. With the train closed, the cops weren't around to protect passengers at the stops, and I realized for the first time that I'd trusted a woman I'd only met earlier this evening with whisking me off to a very local part of the city, with my friends having absolutely no knowledge of my plan. I could disappear forever, and nobody would know where to look for my body.

Isabelle smiled at me but seemed to be giving me a second to soak up my surroundings.

In the not too far distance, a hill rose up from street level to the horizon with gravestones pocking the grass. It was a disorganized graveyard with a hodgepodge of stone crosses, slabs, and tombs. It was clear the burial practices were left to the family to figure out. They had to provide the markers or housing for the dead, which meant some had grandiose above-ground sarcophaguses while others were underground in probably little more than cheap crates.

Across the street was a big, grey warehouse. Painted on the front of the building was a giant white bag that could have been sugar, salt, or flour. I couldn't read the wording on it and probably wouldn't have understood even if I could. Lying on the sidewalk in front of the building was a homeless man and his dog.

"Why here, Isabelle?" I asked.

"This is where the *push button* is," she replied, slinking her arm through mine.

There wasn't a single sound. As if God had vacuum sealed us in this neighborhood, the world seemed to be on mute.

A car sped by and splashed through a puddle, causing me to jump. I hadn't heard it approach and barely heard it leave. It was just there, causing me to jerk away from Isabelle, and then leaving us alone again so I could be on the receiving end of her laughter.

"Don't worry. It is an industrial area," she told me through pauses in her giggles. "I live around the corner, so I thought it would be perfect. That way you can take me home after."

"It's so quiet," I said.

"Do you have any idea what time it is?" she asked. "You have kept me out very late, Mister."

She was right. It had been a long night.

"Children will be getting up for school soon," she said.

A light flickered from behind and with it came the buzz of a neon lamp. I turned to see our destination. The name of the place was outlined in a warm, fiery glow.

Campo Sexo. Interesting.

From the outside, the place looked like a drive-thru Las Vegas wedding chapel. The lit-up sign had a fancy, kind of cheesy font with puckered red lips. We walked toward it and the world no longer felt so dark.

With us both bathed in the sign's warm glow, I asked, "So this is a push?"

"This is a push," she replied. "But not *our* push. Ours is over here."

She walked with me, arm in arm, to the right of what I thought would be our spot for the rest of the evening. Everything else was dark. There weren't any other signs. We rounded a corner and there was nothing but grey slab buildings, an auto shop with a pile of torn-up tires in front of it, and what appeared to be some kind of food shack. *Fonda Delilah* was painted on the front of it with sloppy white paint.

To each side of the closed and locked takeout window, were hand-painted pictures of the eatery's offerings. To the left was a colorful rendition of a cheeseburger – complete with bright orange cheese, green lettuce, and red tomatoes – in an open Styrofoam box. To the right was a tan plate topped with a mountain of white rice and a brown chicken leg with a thigh.

Wind blew a paper cup down the street, like a modern-day tumble-weed blowing across the food shack's path. The clacking of the cup as it bounced echoed through the air.

I'd been uncomfortable before, but now I was concerned.

Horror movies came back to me, none of which happened in an area like this one. *The Hills Have Eyes* took place in a desert, *The Texas Chainsaw Massacre* happened at a Texas farmhouse, and *Halloween*'s setting was a charming suburban neighborhood.

I couldn't shake the feeling that something was wrong. No other sounds were present. It was like we'd stepped out of the vibrant city and into an abandoned wasteland. I imagined five guys leaping out from behind a dumpster and stabbing me to death.

Fuck that shit. Not me.

"Umm, nah, I'm not feeling this," I said. "I don't see anything back here. Let's go back to the casinos."

Isabelle looked down at her feet, her shoulders slumped, saddened that I'd turn my back on her now. "Michael," she said.

"Isabelle, I'm not comfortable with this. I'd really like to go back. We can get a hotel in the casino area."

I wished I'd just rented one in the first place, but no, I had to be a cheapskate.

"No, it's here," Isabelle said. She wasn't the least bit perturbed. "It is. Look. Right over there."

I looked and I couldn't see a thing. It was dark. Just dark.

"I don't see anything. Look, I don't mean to be an asshole, but this is kind of weird."

"Okay," she said.

Well, that was easy. We traveled this far and she's going to give up like that?

"Okay?" I asked. "Okay. Let's find a taxi."

Suddenly lights popped on about halfway down the darkened street. It was a big sign, but I couldn't read it from where I stood.

"See?" she squealed as if she'd just proven to me UFOs exist.

She seemed so proud of herself, and with that sense of pride came a flash of passion that caught me off guard and kept me glued to that dark alley, no longer searching for a way out.

She attacked my mouth, pulling me into her embrace, shoving her tongue past my teeth as her body pushed me against a wall at my back. We rattled against tin siding and rolled around until I was the one leading the assault, lifting her dress, and grabbing that pussy while she reached into my pants and grabbed hold of my cock.

Two frenzied lovers, sparks reignited by the realization that a bed waited for us nearby. This girl was fucking wild, and I found myself wanting nothing more than to get her alone somewhere. Paranoia had almost cost me this night. This girl just wanted to fuck. Who was I to deny her?

Yes, I was thinking with my little head, but sometimes my little head was a genius.

This was not one of those times.

As quickly as that heat took over us both, Isabelle tore it away from me, pulling my hand toward the bright sign awaiting us. She practically skipped the whole way there, and I was close to joining her in that excited strut. I was about to get her alone, and when I did, I was going to pounce on her like a starving man who hadn't eaten in weeks.

We neared the building and the sign finally came into view: *The Love Bug.*

That was it.

So short.

So simple.

So English.

The script was written in an erotic looking font and beside it was the neon outline of one love bug fucking another from behind, doggy style. It was one of those animated, motion signs, and this bug was really giving it to her. It reminded me of the sign in the movie *Porky's* with the female pig lifting her skirt for the male. Only this one was much more vulgar.

Nice.

I laughed under my breath, feeling much better and no longer doubting Isabelle's decision to bring me here. It was perfect. The darkness of the street behind me faded away. Sure, it was odd that the sign had suddenly come to life as we'd rounded the corner and approached, but I figured someone must have realized the sign was off and hit the switch. It was a coincidence. A strange coincidence, but stranger shit had definitely happened.

Get out of your head. You're with a beautiful woman. Make her yours tonight.

That's when I decided to let go and let this happen. Isabelle had brought me here, she'd been right about the place so far, and she'd shown me no reason not to trust her.

"Come on," she said.

I allowed her to pull me toward the door.

3

As we approached, I saw past the blinding light of the neon sign and realized it was a large, two-story structure. Palm trees lined the bottom floor, illuminated by the blinking sign. It was a pretty sight. It had a beachy kind of vibe. If this were an oceanside bar, it would be the perfect atmosphere to sit and enjoy a few beers.

The second floor looked more like an office building with a large floor-to-ceiling, pitch-black glass window looking out over the street.

Is someone up there looking at us now? Up there taking bets on how long I'll last with this beautiful Latina?

In the U.S., there were so many laws to prohibit spying on customers, but I knew very little of Panama, and I wondered how easy it would be to get away with filming hotel rooms and uploading the action to porn websites.

It has to happen somewhere. How many discreet sexual hideaways around the world are selling your heated moments to the highest bidder?

Isabelle, who'd apparently visited this place before, yanked me out of my negative thoughts as she led me toward the front door. This was a fact that hadn't dawned on me until now. How did she even know about this place? Obviously, someone had brought her here.

Don't judge her. She's had ex-boyfriends like you've had ex-girl-friends. Did you think you were taking a virgin to a hotel to fuck tonight?

At first, it seemed like we were walking toward a main entrance door like at any other hotel, but then I realized there wasn't a door. There was only a wall beneath the sign. To the right was a driveway that led up a small hill and disappeared behind another wall that seemed to be acting as a barrier of sorts, like it was blocking the world behind it from view.

"Up here," she said as she led me up the driveway.

We ascended the incline and disappeared behind the wall, which was definitely meant to give privacy to anyone visiting this *push button,* and then we walked beneath an archway wide enough for a car to drive through. As we rounded the corner, the driveway opened up to a long parking lot at least a hundred yards in length.

A long line of garage doors was to our left. To our right was the perimeter wall.

"What is this?" I asked.

"I'll show you," she promised, giving my hand another squeeze.

We turned left and Isabelle held out a hand, gesturing at the doors. It was a long wall of garage door after garage door after garage door. I'd never seen anything like it. It looked like we'd just walked into a storage site.

"Choose a door," Isabelle said.

"Any door?"

"They're all very similar," she said. "The ones on the end are the most expensive because they have a hot tub."

I didn't want a hot tub. It was hard for me to imagine anyone cleaning them after each use. By now, it was probably a nasty human soup inside one of their Jacuzzis.

"I don't think we need a hot tub, do you?" I asked.

She giggled. "No. I think we will be hot enough."

When I didn't answer right away, she added, "Usually people come here in a car."

That made sense.

"Which one would you like?" she asked.

"I um…"

They all looked the same to me. I had no idea what was in store. How could I choose? It felt like I was playing another casino game.

Will you hit the jackpot, or will you strike out?

"This one I guess," I said as I pointed at the third garage from the entrance, the result of the genius *eenie meenie miney mo* strategy of my youth.

Isabelle stood up on her toes and kissed my cheek before pulling me in the direction of our garage.

I got an odd feeling in my gut for the second time this night. If this place had been out on the main drag where I could at least hear cars driving by or taxis honking or dogs barking, I would have felt better.

We walked into the garage and it was no different from any other I'd been in, minus the tools and shelves full of auto parts found in most of the ones back home. This was only an empty room with bare sandy brown walls. An old oil stain decorated the ground. In the far-left corner, there was a door. Next to it was a small intercom and a panel with one button.

"So, this is it?" I asked, my voice bouncing around the empty room. "This is where the magic happens?"

"You are funny," Isabelle said. "Of course not." She walked toward the door in the back and pointed at a sign at its center. "See?"

I stepped closer. The sign, professionally stenciled on a wooden plaque, read: $12 por 2 horas, $20 por 4. Below the sign was a chrome mail slot.

Isabelle shrugged her shoulders. It was an awkward moment. Would I need two hours or four or more? I was still a little uneasy about being here in the first place. Would I want to stay at all?

Isabelle pushed the button on the wall and the garage door creaked shut.

I looked back and watched it, piece by piece, descend from the ceiling to the concrete, locking me in. Locking *us* in.

"*Push button?*" I asked, finally getting the name of the place.

She smiled. "*Push button.*"

"Original."

"Yes," she agreed. "Kind of like *gas* station."

Smartass.

She had a point though. What were they supposed to call this place? Pussy palace? It reminded me of a sign I once passed back home that read: *Realtor Realtors.* I chuckled and it felt good to finally let out some of the nervous energy.

"You are happy with me," Isabelle said.

Is that a question or a statement?

It didn't matter. I *was* happy with her, and I found the way she'd worded it endearing. I nodded.

The garage door finally reached the bottom with a loud clunk that brought back that icy chill from before. I'd never had an issue with enclosed spaces, but I didn't like feeling locked in.

All was silent again. Eerily silent. I didn't like it.

Then Isabelle hugged me from behind, resting her chin on my back and reaching out to intertwine her fingers at my stomach. It was a cute gesture and made me feel like we'd been dating for a long time.

SQUEAK, the mail slot swung open, causing us both to flinch.

I hopped back, nearly knocking Isabelle over.

The mail slot slammed into the fully open position and was held there by a woman's hand. I could only see her blood-red nail polish peeking through the narrow, rectangular space.

The fuck?

I didn't know what to do. What was going on?

"You have to give her money," Isabelle said. "How long will we stay?"

"Umm…"

Isabelle smiled and relieved me of the pressure by calling out, "*Dos horas por favor.*"

Then she said to me, "Just hand her the money. She will give you change after."

"Two hours you said?"

"Yes," she replied. "Twelve dollars. Why? You want more time with me?" The question made her sound like a prostitute, but then she smiled and said, "If we want to stay longer, we can pay more after."

I pulled a twenty out of my wallet and put it through the slot. The woman took it and disappeared.

All was quiet again.

"This is weird," I said.

"What is?" Isabelle asked.

"All of it."

"These places are very popular in Panama. Um... lovers... they come here for alone time."

"I get it. It's just odd, you know? Not seeing anyone. It's very mysterious."

"Don't worry. You will get your change when we go inside."

"I'm not worried about that. It's just weird."

"It's for discretion, I believe is the word you say. A lot of cheaters come here with their mistresses. Their car is safe inside the garage, nobody can see, nobody can report later. It's all done in secret."

CLICK the door popped open and squeaked as it swung on its hinges. The light was on in the room. The sounds of a heavy door shutting and locking came from somewhere inside.

"We can go in now," Isabelle said.

4

Isabelle went in ahead of me, pushing the door all the way open. It wasn't what I expected. It was basically a Days Inn but kinkier. I closed and locked the door behind me and did a quick survey of the room.

The bed was probably queen size with a thin cheap comforter draped over it, an ugly flowered design, and a couple of those rock-hard pillows you always find at ratty hotels. The color scheme looked like something out of the 70s or early 80s. Mostly orange and brown with an ugly triangle pattern on the carpet.

The bathroom was to the right and half of the wall between the two rooms was see-through, with the glass portion giving me a perfect view of the shower stall. I could sit on the bed and watch Isabelle shower. Or, she could watch me.

Okay, that's hot.

A TV was bolted to the wall across from the foot of the bed, over a dresser.

On the nightstand was a laminated piece of paper. I picked it up and it was a sex toy menu with prices next to each item. A vibrator, a bigger vibrator, a fucking gigantic vibrator. A cock ring, sensual oils, a strap-on kit. Whips, cuffs, floggers, and even knives. The list went on and on, catering to the slightly kinky all the way to the totally twisted.

At the bottom was a list of alcoholic beverages complete with combos. For forty-five dollars, you could get a candle, a lighter, and a bottle of vodka. For eighty-five you could get a bottle of champagne and an alien tentacle-shaped dildo. I'd done some kinky shit in my time, but I wasn't about to ask Isabelle if she was in the mood to have an alien appendage inside her and we definitely weren't putting it up my ass, so I figured we could do without.

Also, on the nightstand was an old rotary phone, and I realized we could have all the toys we wanted delivered to our door with a quick phone call.

Slapping the laminated menu against my open palm, I glanced back at Isabelle and saw her standing in front of a wall-mounted TV, playing with the remote control. She hit the "on" button and the screen lit up. I was still watching her when I heard the typical porn sounds. Upbeat music to a cry of, *"Oh, fuck! Yes, put it in my ass!"*

My attention went to the TV where I could see that he was indeed putting it in her ass while *she* tongued another girl's clit.

Classy place. Glad to see they watch the same cheesy porn in Central America. And in English.

On the dresser, below the TV, was a plastic pouch with clean towels and a condom packed inside.

The concept of this place was brilliant, and I wondered why we didn't have *push buttons* back home. Discreet places for lovers to meet up, hide their car in a garage, buy some sex toys, watch porn, and even have a condom provided for the extremely low price of $20 for four hours? These places would make a killing.

I was contemplating opening one of these businesses myself when I looked at Isabelle and saw the way she watched the porno in front of her. She stood with her legs closed, raised up slightly on the toes of one foot, a finger in her mouth. She looked so fucking sexy.

She noticed I was staring and then pointed a finger toward the sky. I followed her gesture, looking up, and saw the ceiling was completely mirrored. I'd never been in a room like this before.

She smiled and bit her finger.

Holy fuck.

My heart sped up. I realized I was anxious, or nervous, or a combination of the two. I wasn't frightened like I'd been out in the garage. I was just so fucking horny. I'd been with maybe twenty women in my life and had only been this nervous with the first. Why was I so fucking turned on by this gorgeous Latin beauty? What made her different from all the others?

"You like me?" she asked.

I couldn't control my breathing. Anxiety was building up inside and I knew if I didn't unleash it on her, I'd fucking pass out in a second. This was too much anticipation.

"I want you," I said.

She tilted her head to the side, her hair over one shoulder exposing her smooth neck on the other side. When she smiled, her lip lifted only enough to show her teeth, and she was the sexiest fucking thing I'd ever seen in my life.

"In my country, men take what they want," she said.

She took her sweater off and tossed it to the floor.

It was the first time I'd seen her in bright light, without that sweater over her, and I realized her shoulders and arms were covered in tattoos. Flowers, birds, and strange symbols. I'd always been a sucker for tattoos, and these were exotic and sexy as hell. What I'd thought were just a couple of tats sticking out from her top earlier at the restaurant had turned in to a tapestry of art, a mural of "fuck me now."

I wanted her, and as she'd said, in her country, men took what they wanted. I was in her country, and I needed to take her.

Rushing at her, I grabbed her by her waist and the back of her head and kissed her hard, no longer worried about a cab driver spying on us. I just wanted to taste her, to devour her, to be inside her in any way possible. I wanted my tongue, my fingers, and my cock… all of them inside her.

She shoved me away for a second and I was stunned. Then she winked, pulled off her dress, and let it fall to her feet.

Her tits were propped up in her bra, lace cups that were slightly see-through, giving me just a hint of the big, dark nipples that lay beneath.

Her belly was smooth, not muscular, but perfect, and a swirl of ivy stretched around from her ribcage, leading to a red flower that encircled her belly button.

Black lace panties covered her pussy but were see-through enough for me to catch a glimpse of the crease. My cock throbbed in my pants, my chest heaved up and down, and saliva built up in my mouth. An animalistic lust coursed through my veins.

She walked past me and crawled onto the bed, making sure to put her ass up in front of me so I could see the small pouch at the bottom of her panties where her succulent pussy was poised for the taking.

With a glance over her shoulder, she watched as I reached down, grabbed the width of my cock, picked it up, and adjusted it. Her pursed lips and the way she said, "Mmm," told me she liked what she saw. At the head of the bed, she turned and sat down, putting her back against the headboard as she motioned for me to come to her. "Take off your clothes and come sit with me."

I turned off the lights and stared at her beautiful body in the flicker of the TV glow. The sounds of the woman getting pounded on screen intensified the moment.

"Ohhhh shit!" she woman on TV cried. "You're so fucking good!"

The other woman cried, "Yeah, don't stop. Eat my pussy."

And during all this, Isabelle's eyes were glued on me.

I pulled my shirt over my head and she smiled.

"And your... pants," she said with a point of her finger, ordering me out of them.

I slid off my shoes and pulled down my pants, not stripper-like as I didn't have the talent, but frustrated, because I was tired of the games. I kicked my pants to the side. I was only in my boxers now, and my cock was pressed so hard against them that the head found its own way out of the hole in the front, peeking out at her.

"Oh," she said as she put a hand to her chest.

I dropped my boxers and my cock sprang to life, standing straight up, ready to be eaten by whatever hole she had in mind.

She patted the bed in front of her.

"Come sit in front of me and let's watch the show."

I climbed onto the bed on all fours, watching her the whole time, my cock dangling between my legs, jerking with each move forward. Her eyes were drawn to it and her mouth was agape. She wanted it. She wanted me.

This is going to be epic.

But I didn't give it to her at first. She wanted me to sit in front of her, so I did. My back to her chest. She put her hands on my ribs, digging her nails into my flesh just a little, and whispered. "Come closer. Lean into me."

I slid back a little and she pulled me into her. I rested my head on her shoulder.

"Just a moment," she said.

She pushed me forward for a second, then pulled me back again and I felt her bare nipples against my back. She held her bra out so I could see she'd removed it. It fell onto the bed next to me.

Her tits were so soft against my back. I savored the feel of her against me as I watched the naked romp on the screen in front of me. Then Isabelle's face was on my shoulder as she leaned forward to watch it with me.

"You have a pretty penis," she said.

"Everything about you is pretty," I replied, hating the cheesy words the moment they left my mouth, but she didn't seem to mind them.

She reached around my lap and touched my balls, sliding her fingernails under them. My ass clenched as I lifted slightly off the bed. My heart raced. She moved her hand to my cock, lightly running her fingers over it as if learning everything about it by touch. She played with the vein at its underbelly, ran her thumb along the top, and then paused at my head, clinching two fingers at its base, and then moving them over it in a circular motion.

I was so fucking sensitive I thought I might scream as she kept brushing her hand over the head of my cock. My nerves were on fire.

"Fuck," I said as I turned my face, trying to find hers.

"You like it?" she asked.

"I love it."

And she moved down my cock, finally stroking it, making it hers. She owned it at that moment. She squeezed and jerked up and down. On the screen, a guy was getting a blowjob. I wanted one.

"This is boring," Isabelle said. "We can find something better to watch."

She switched and jacked me off with her left hand as she reached for the remote with her right. I watched as she pointed it at the TV and pressed a code, #2991. Then she pressed the channel up button.

Why the code?

I pulled away from her for a second and turned the best I could to see her.

"You pushed a lot of buttons just to change the channel," I said.

She squinted her eyes and cocked her head to the side. Then she grinned.

"Oh, that… that is a Panama code. It unlocks TVs in hotel rooms. We use them at the casino too."

Strange.

I was staying in a hotel room and I never had to enter #2991 to watch TV or change the channel. I'd never seen my buddies do it either.

Isabelle stopped pushing buttons when she found a giant orgy scene in a room where everything was red. Red mattresses, red couches, red pillows. At least five couples lay all over each other, crisscrossed, one lover draped over the other in some way, as each person busied him or herself with another. It was wild, but my attention was pulled from the screen when Isabelle slid out from behind me.

She got on her hands and knees and crawled around to my lap. My eyes never left her as she lifted up and arched her back while twisting her hair into a bun. Somehow, she pinned it there, and her face was so pure, so flawless with her hair pulled away from it.

She opened her mouth and giggled. Her tongue glistened in the TV light as she dangled it down above the tip of my cock.

Her eyes were locked on mine as she reached out, grabbed the base of my cock, and licked me, once again hitting those nerves.

"Your mind is in the wrong place, baby," she said. "Bring it back to me."

She licked me again, her dark eyes locked on mine, her naked tits hanging down as she hovered over me, her tongue out like a she-wolf stalking its prey.

"Fuck," I said. "You are so fucking gorgeous."

And that was her cue to take it all in. She closed her eyes, opened her mouth wide, and sank down, wrapping her soft lips around me. I felt the tip of my cock hit her tonsils. And she didn't gag. She just raised her face and then lowered it again and it felt like she was swirling her tongue around too, giving special attention to the head with each lift.

She opened her eyes and stared at me, keeping them locked on mine as she lowered over my cock. I watched myself disappear inside her mouth and then slide out while she squinted and watched me hungrily. She rose and fell rhythmically, with her nails digging into my balls and one finger inching closer to my ass. She was in total fucking control.

I was in heaven. It was easily the best blowjob I'd ever had. She was fucking me with her mouth, making me forget about everything else.

Behind her, the movie changed tone. It was no longer the whimsical 70s-like orgy from before with the goofy music, the colorful outfits, and the pigtails. It was darker. A man hung from the ceiling, chains around his wrists, completely naked.

Blood ran down his chest and over the face of a woman who was sucking his cock.

It was a freaky movie. Creepy. But I couldn't concentrate on it with Isabelle sucking me the way she was. She'd picked up her pace and my hand shot up to grab her hair. I wanted to have some control of the situation. I gripped her hair and pulled it tight. She gasped.

I dug in and cranked back on her roots. It had to hurt.

"Anh, uh…" she cried as she kept working me.

Her finger found my asshole and touched me, causing me to buck and cry out. She laughed and pressed the pad of her finger against me once more as she continued to rise and fall. She never entered me, but she put enough pressure there to let me know if I tried to control the situation again, she'd go there.

So many sensations washed over me. A wave of dizziness hit me, and I leaned back.

I'd forgotten the mirrored ceiling. Seeing her suck my cock like that was strange. I felt like I was the one on film, like I was part of the porn, and it was fucking brilliant.

More than anything, I was enjoying the sight of Isabelle bent over on top of me. Her bare back was so smooth, her tattoos crawling their way down her shoulders and onto her back. Ivy and flowers and more birds. It was so fucking sexy.

Her ass was propped up and fantastic. Her black panties rode up into her crack. The bun on top of her head was starting to unravel and some strands of her long, black hair hung down, adding a sexy messiness to her perfection. The woman was un-fucking-believable.

The sight of her was too much. I needed her right then and there. No more foreplay.

She jumped a little as I grabbed her arm. I'd scared her. I grabbed her other arm and rolled her over, so I was on top of her. Her tits didn't give in to gravity the way real tits did, and I finally knew they were fake. But they were beautiful. Her areolas were so dark and her nipples so fucking erect.

Her eyes, black in the darkness, watched me, and I wanted to lose myself in them. I wanted to climb inside her and join her in her excellence. Her soul just seemed like such a perfect place to be.

"Are you going to fuck me now?" she asked. "Or are you too much of a pussy?"

Where the fuck did that come from?

She bit her bottom lip, and that was it. I reached down, grabbed her panties, and tore the fabric clean off. I ripped open a spot for me to insert my cock. She squealed and laughed as I threw the tattered panties onto the floor.

I looked down at her and she giggled, loving the mind games, and clearly knowing she'd struck a nerve.

"I don't think you have it in you to fuck me," she said.

"No?"

"No, you are a pussy."

"I'm a pussy?"

I shoved her legs open, gripped the base of my cock, and shoved it inside her hard. She cried out in pain. She was wet, but I was large enough that it didn't go in easily. Her arms fell back to the mattress and her eyes rolled back as I pulled out of her and thrust into her again.

"I'm a pussy?" I asked again.

"You're a... you're a..."

She couldn't get the words out, so I pulled out of her and crammed myself in again.

"I'm a pussy?" I repeated.

Two more thrusts and she was back to normal, given new life, and she was wilder than ever. Whatever pain she'd felt before had dissipated and now she only wanted to be fucked.

"Fuck my pussy," she demanded.

"Like this?" I asked as I pulled out and rammed it inside her again.

"Fuck me!" she yelled as she lashed out and slapped me.

It stung and I didn't realize she'd slashed me with her nails until I saw the blood dripping on her chest. That infuriated me even more. I picked her up off the bed and slammed her down on it, my cock driving into her as she bounced off the mattress.

She howled. She laughed. She begged for more.

So, I gave her more. I picked her up again and drove into her on the way down.

"Oh fuck!" she screamed. "Holy fuck! Yes!"

I stood and picked her up. She wrapped her legs around me. I slammed her against the wall and launched up on my toes, skewering her with my cock. Her mouth hung open lazily.

"Unh, unh, unh, unh..." she moaned each time I lifted up into her.

"You're a fucking animal," I yelled as I kept plugging away.

She giggled, her laughter coming out in breathy gasps.

Then she switched to Spanish and said something in a deeper, rougher voice. An angry voice. The only word I caught was *demonio*.

"What?" I asked as I kept driving into her.

She repeated herself, her voice getting even lower. She growled and it sounded guttural. Scary. Inside her pussy I felt movement, like muscles were squeezing me, massaging me, pulling on me.

She laughed. "Yes! I'm your animal, baby!"

Her voice was normal again, and her pussy continued to massage me from the inside. It was the most glorious thing I'd ever felt. I'd never had a woman like this before. She buried her face in my shoulder and bit down, drawing blood. It leaked down my shoulder and over my chest. She pulled her face away and tore a chunk of flesh out.

Searing pain hit me, and more blood ran down my chest and stomach.

A man screamed in agony on the TV screen. A woman cackled. The man kept screaming in pain.

"Fuck me!" Isabelle demanded. "I'm your animal, baby! I'm your fucking animal. I'm your demon-lover!"

She suddenly pushed off the wall and I toppled over, falling straight back to the floor on my back with a thud. She landed on me in a dangerous way. She fell onto my cock so hard I felt like I must've shoved all the way up into her stomach. She screamed so loudly and with so much agony I immediately tried to pull out of her, but I couldn't.

Her pussy held me there, squeezing my cock, still tugging on me.

"Don't pull out of me, baby," she begged. "I can handle it."

"Isabelle," I said. "Wait—"

"—Come inside my cunt, you fucking pussy!" she cut me off in that deep, throaty howl. This wasn't the innocent sweetheart I'd met at the restaurant.

She didn't stop fucking me. Even with the pain she was in, she rode me. She lifted off me and slammed down on top of me, lifted and smashed, lifted and smashed. She was uncontrollable.

"Fuck me, damn you," she screamed. "Fuck me!"

I was trying to. She was insatiable. She had a desire, a thirst I just couldn't seem to quench. She turned around, barely pulling me out in the process, and rode me reverse cowgirl right there on the dirty floor.

You're not wearing a condom. You never stopped to put one on.

It hadn't occurred to me that I wasn't wearing one. I'd been drunk in her seduction and hadn't even considered it. Now, it was too late.

"I should get a condom," I told her.

"Nooooooooo!" she howled, her voice coming out like that of three different women of varying ages.

"Fill my cunt with your seed!" the voice of an old lady belted from her gut as Isabelle dug her nails into my sides and pulled, her claws slicing my skin.

"Ah, fuck!" I screamed, trying to throw her off me but she was stronger than me and she held me down.

"Your cock is mine!" a young woman with what sounded like a New York accent cried.

"Baby, be with me," Isabelle's sweet Spanish accent returned.

For the first time since entering the room, I was fucking terrified. Blood seeped from my head, my shoulder, and my new wounds at both sides of my ribcage where she'd cut right through me with inhuman like claws.

"I'm fucking cut bad," I said as I finally rallied enough strength to launch her off me. She fell to the side and I got to my feet as quickly as I could. I looked around the room and at all the blood on the floor.

Where the fuck are your clothes? Get your clothes and get out of here.

My cock pulsated. I was still so hard. Glancing over my shoulder, I saw Isabelle sitting on the floor, naked, slathered in my blood as she looked down at the carpet, sadness on her face. I'd ruined our good time.

No, are you fucking crazy? She's not normal! Get out of here!

But my eyes were drawn to her tits, to her erect nipples, to that thatch of stubble between her legs. I wasn't finished yet. I could simply finish and then go. I could do that much, right? I was almost there, almost done.

Michael, get out of here. Don't be stupid.

Isabelle lazily stood up and then plopped onto the bed. "I don't know what I've done to make you treat me like this," she whined. "I thought you liked me."

"Oh, God, Isabelle. I do like you."

"You don't act like it. You were only using me for my body."

"No, never."

"You are a fucking pussy," she said. "You use me and then don't even finish me so I can enjoy it too."

"Isabelle, I'm hurt," I said.

She looked at me and shook her head. She lowered her gaze to my cock and smiled.

"You're not hurt that badly, baby," she said.

"I'm bleeding all over the place."

My hand went to the rip in my shoulder. My face was bleeding too. Blood ran down both my sides and over my thighs from her most recent cuts.

"When you love someone, you bleed for them," she said.

That's crazy. You see? Get out of here.

But it seemed to make so much sense at the time. She laughed and stood up at the foot of the bed, circling one nipple with her fingernail. She let the nail slice her skin enough to send blood trickling down.

"I would bathe in your blood, Michael," she said, "and I would have you bathe in mine."

It excited me. It shouldn't have, but she'd done something to me. She'd awoken some kind of hunger. I'd never been with anyone so demented, so wild, but as much as it had scared me a few seconds ago, it drove me wild now. I wanted her more. She was right, I hadn't finished off my woman.

And she hadn't finished me off.

"I thought you were man enough to tame my pussy, baby," she said in a sweet voice. She giggled. "Guess not. Maybe I should order a toy and finish myself."

Again, my temper flared. I ran at her and through gritted teeth hissed, "Bend the fuck over right fucking now."

"Mmm," she replied as I bent her over the bed and crammed my cock into her pussy again. I gripped her waist and crashed into her. I looked up at the ceiling and laughed. I cackled. I fucking laughed maniacally, loving the sight of the skin of her ass rippling as I pounded it from behind.

My blood splashed onto her back and instead of being worried about my well-being, I just wanted to punish her, to fuck her harder. I put my hand to my face and found it slick with blood. I wiped my hand through it and slapped her ass.

My handprint was wet and red, and I slapped her again.

"Oh shit, yeah!" she screamed.

I slapped her again.

"Fucking hit me!"

A welt was forming on her ass. I slapped it again. I was fucking the shit out of her.

I grabbed her hair and yanked her head back as I kept smashing into her. Her tits shook, and I watched as her eyes slammed shut and her mouth fell open. She was going to come. And I was going to fuck her through it.

"This fucking pussy is mine," I yelled. "You hear that? You think I'm a fucking pussy? This is a fucking pussy and I want you to come. I want you to fucking come! You hear me?"

"Yes... ooooh... yes!"

"Yes what?"

"Yes... I... hear... you... just... keep... fuck... ing... me... please!" her voice stuttering out in syllables each time my cock drove into her.

But then she pulled away from me, spun, and slapped the shit out of me. Her nails clawed at my face again, bringing more blood running down my chin. A short stint of confusion hit me, and then she yanked on my arm, pulling me back onto the mattress where she threw me onto my back with more strength than any woman her size should have.

She grabbed my cock and snarled at me as she shoved me inside her and began riding me again.

Isabelle rolled her hips and got into a rhythm, a strange rhythm that went along to the chanting that was coming from the TV. Murmurs, music, and screaming sounded off behind me. I looked over my shoulder, back at the screen, and saw the man in chains shrieking as the woman cut his chest with a knife.

I looked down at my own chest and at the blood that had pooled there from my cuts. I reached up to touch the slashes and they were tender. They burned. She'd cut me bad. I touched her back and left a bloody handprint. My shoulder was pouring blood and I felt weak.

My temporary rage had blinded me to the reason I'd pulled away from her in the first place. She'd fucked me up badly.

"Isabelle," I said. "I'm bleeding too much. I think I'm gonna pass out."

She ignored me and kept fucking me. I tried to pull away once more but that grip inside her pussy was back. The muscles inside her squeezed me, loosening and then tightening over me, holding my cock in its clutch. Her pussy was strong, and it squeezed me so tight it hurt. She rode me so vigorously I felt myself about to come. I couldn't stop it.

"I think I'm almost there," she said, her voice coming out as the sweet Isabelle from before. "Yes, I'm there again. Don't you dare pull away from me this time, you fucking pussy!"

"Did you hear me? I'm cut. I'm bleeding a lot."

"I'm gonna come. Make me come, baby."

I grabbed her hair and tried pulling her off me. It hurt like hell, like I might snap in half. It was like she was welded to me. My cock couldn't leave her, and that sensation continued, that warm stroking of my shaft from inside her.

Fuck. It hurts but it feels so fucking good.

I was bleeding all over the place, but I couldn't stop fucking her. I didn't want to stop fucking her.

"Come for me, baby," Isabelle begged.

"I don't want—"

"—Give me your fucking seed!" the voice that came out of her could have been shouted from the pits of hell. It was monstrous, hoarse, and sounded like so many voices wrapped up into one.

I fell back to the mattress and stared up at the mirrored ceiling. Her beautiful naked body flashed between the lovely Isabelle, and something dark, black, and covered in hair. Its face was melted, and on its head were chopped, jagged horns. Her feet at my sides were replaced by tar-black hooves. The hairy beast road me with wild abandon, thrashing around on top of me.

I screamed and it rode me harder.

It flashed back to Isabelle, who stared up at the ceiling too, smiling at me, her mouth open, lips over her teeth, as she gave in to the massive orgasm beginning to rock through her body.

She screamed with so much enjoyment that it seemed to signal her pussy to grip me harder. It felt like ten tiny hands were inside of her, all working together, pulling on my cock, and I was about to come.

I didn't want to.

But I was going to come.

I was… I was fucking going to.

Blood poured over me.

She flashed back to the dark demon in the mirror. Its face looked at me too, and its eyes were pitch black. Its tongue slithered out and was forked. It sneered, wrinkling up its nose, and it hissed. "Give us your seed."

"No!" I yelled, but I was coming.

My cock jerked inside the thing.

It flashed back to Isabelle, and she smiled at me, her tits rising and falling as she continued to ride me.

"Yes, baby. That's it," she told me. "Come for me."

As I shot my load inside her, whatever was gripping me down there sped up, like it couldn't get enough. It feverishly sucked on me like her pussy had its own mouth and it was drinking me dry, lapping up every drop.

"What are you?" I asked as it continued to pull my seed from me.

"I'm Isabelle, baby," she replied. "What do you mean?"

"I'm hurt," I whispered, slapping a bloody hand against her back to try to push her off.

But she kept going, the hands kept massaging, and my cock remained hard.

I was still coming.

A new wave of orgasm hit me, and I clenched my ass cheeks and lifted into her as my cock pulsated once more and felt like it might burst. I cried out, never having experienced a second orgasm like this so soon after the first.

"Holy fuck!" I yelled and she kept grinding at me from the inside.

"I feel you," she said, giggling.

Isabelle held onto her hair with one hand, so I could see her beautiful face. My blood was smeared across her chin and cheek, but she didn't wipe it away.

"I feel you inside me," she added, "wriggling in there, alive in there and... and..."

Her face wrinkled up and her mouth shot open again. A wail leapt from her throat. "I'm coming again!" She screamed. She was about to come hard. "Ahh! Shit!" she growled. Her voice transformed again to that deep, disgusting groan. "I'm coming. Don't stop. Ohhhhh!"

This time I felt her. Whatever had been squeezing me inside her stopped. Like the muscles had seized up and backed away, and a new sensation flowed forth. Warm liquid poured over me and ran down my cock, dripped over my balls and pooled under my ass on the mattress. She squirted and drenched me.

"Was that?" I asked.

"I came with you," she replied.

"I didn't think that was possible... not like that."

"This was nice," she said and then fell down onto my chest.

She laughed.

I didn't.

I could only see that demon on top of me, and as her naked body lay against mine, flesh against flesh, I wanted to push her away, but I couldn't.

My eyes fluttered lazily and then slammed shut.

Was that real? Was she a... was that a... was that a monster? A demon? You're being ridiculous. You were seeing things because of the loss of blood.

The loss of blood. I couldn't get up, I couldn't move, and I passed out.

5

It had to be close to dawn when I woke up. Isabelle had rolled off me, and I found myself lying on my back in a semi-hungover state.

"Where are you going?" I asked, my eyes on the mirrored ceiling, taking in the sight of my own naked and dirty form. Dried blood caked my torso, but the wounds didn't seem quite as deep as I'd originally thought.

"To take a shower, baby," she said. "You left me really messy."

"I left you messy?"

I glanced to the side and watched her magnificent, naked form sashay out of the room and into the bathroom. I'd had a horrible dream about a hairy demon riding me.

It was a dream, right?

The cuts on my body weren't a dream. Was the rest of it? Had I simply had too much to drink or lost too much blood? I rolled over and looked at the carpet. It was indeed stained red. Could blood loss cause those kinds of hallucinations? Anything seemed possible. Anything but actually seeing this Latin beauty transform into a demon while in the midst of the best sex I'd ever had in my life.

What would it be like to stick around Panama for a while? Could you have a relationship with this girl?

47

Her demonic form flashed behind my closed eyelids and jolted my eyes open. I rubbed at them.

You're hallucinating again, man. Cut that shit out. Isabelle is nothing but sweetness. A little bit aggressive in bed, but what man doesn't like that?

Isabelle was the hottest, most animalistic girl I'd ever experienced. She was the girl you took home to mom and then bent over the hood of your car in the driveway after. She was the sweet housewife and the dirty whore. She was everything a man wanted.

With her out of the room, I sat up and pulled on my boxers. I needed to get in the shower too, but I was afraid my wounds were too fresh.

The water might fuck you up bad.

I plopped back onto the bed and watched the strange porn in front of me. It was sick.

A man chewed on a woman's nipple, and it looked like he was really eating it. Blood ran from his mouth and the woman was crying out in pain.

"For fuck's sake. What's wrong with these people?" I asked.

Isabelle couldn't hear me over the sound of the shower. I looked back and watched her through the window. She saw me spying on her, blew me a kiss, and smacked the window, leaving her palm print on the steaming glass.

On TV, the woman kept crying as the man continued to chew on her. The sound of her begging, pleading voice pulled my attention away from Isabelle's shower. I reached for the remote and tried to change the channel. Nothing happened. I tried again. It lit up but the TV remained on the same channel. Then I remembered the code. I pushed #2991 and then the up button and the channel changed.

A woman rode a guy on screen.

I pushed *up* again.

A guy fucked another guy in the ass.

I pushed *up* again.

A man dressed like a ninja fucked a circus clown.

I pressed *up* again.

I don't know what I was looking for, but I kept changing channels. So much porn, so much odd variety, but nothing as bad as the guy chewing on the nipple. This was all regular pornography and nothing else. No normal TV shows. No news segments, sitcoms, or infomercials. Just fucking… on every channel.

The screen went black. I pushed *up* again.

Black.

Again.

Black.

Again.

A strange show flashed onto the screen. *An older man, maybe sixty years old, was in an empty room. He was frightened and was frantically pacing back and forth. He walked to a door at the corner of the room and banged on it.*

Written at the lower right corner of the screen were the words: *Diablo Snuff.*

"Help me!" the man yelled. "Somebody open the fucking door. This isn't funny. If it's money you want… I have money. Please."

"What is this?" I asked aloud.

I looked over once again at Isabelle and saw her washing her hair. I thought about joining her. It would beat watching this bullshit TV.

The man on the screen stole my attention. He cried out as he moved to each wall in the room and banged with a closed fist. "Please… just let me out!" He went to the bathroom door and banged on it. It too was locked. "Let me the fuck out of here!"

Then a spout of some sort came out of the ceiling, like fire control sprinklers, and spit something wet down onto the man. He covered his face.

"What is that? What are you…"

He sniffed and then started to scream.

"No! No, please! Let me out of here! I won't tell anyone!"

Something came out of the wall, like a small box, and a flame shot out.

Suddenly there was fire everywhere. The man screamed as he fell to his knees and rolled around, the relentless flames covering him. He stood, ran into a wall, and fell back down to the floor.

His screams were so loud. So real. This wasn't acting. It couldn't be.

"What the fuck?" I said aloud. "Isabelle, what kind of shit is on this TV?"

Again, she couldn't hear me over the shower.

I entered the code and pushed the *up* button again.

Another room. This one was just like the previous, completely empty, bare walls with a bare floor. No furniture at all. This guy looked really young, probably just past the eighteen-year mark. He was walking around the room, his hands in his pockets.

At the bottom right of the screen were the words: *Diablo Snuff.*

What the fuck is Diablo Snuff?

I returned my gaze to the man on the screen.

He spoke a language I wasn't familiar with. He didn't look to be too worried but was calling out a woman's name. Anna Maria. He kept saying it over and over again.

As I watched the man pace back and forth, I paid closer attention to the room, specifically the door where I saw a mail slot.

I looked over at the mail slot on the door to my room. I looked back at the TV and saw the door was in the same exact location. I noticed the angle of the camera in relation to the door and looked over my shoulder and up at the air conditioning vent.

Is there a camera in there?

I glanced back at the man on the screen once more and then back at the air vent. It was the exact angle from which he was being recorded. I thought about the garages outside. Three of them had been closed. Just like mine was now.

I pulled on my jeans and reached for my shoes. I slid them on without socks. I just wanted to get the fuck out of there. I didn't even grab my shirt.

Isabelle was still in the shower. I looked over at the clear window expecting to see her beautiful form being soaped up. The shower was empty, but the water was on. Isabelle was nowhere in sight.

"Isabelle?" I called out.

"Anna Maria!" yelled the guy on the TV.

"Isabelle?"

"Anna Maria!"

I walked to the bathroom and slid it open. As I did, I looked once more at the TV.

The young man who'd seemed so pleasant moments before was starting to freak out. He was yelling in his language. He pounded on the walls around him and banged against the bathroom door. He was trapped.

Then small holes opened up in the walls around him.

The look on his face was pure terror. He glanced up at the ceiling and opened his mouth to scream when a blade shot down and skewered him through his throat.

A sharp steel spike shot through his stomach, another through his right knee, and a third through his neck. Then more blades came at him until the man looked like a bloody pincushion.

He couldn't even fall to the floor as the long blades held him up. He'd become a morbid statue in a demented gallery.

"The fuck?" I yelled. "Isabelle!"

I was just about to step into the bathroom when the door slammed on my foot in its attempt to auto-lock.

I screamed as the bones in my foot shattered.

The door, which had looked to be wooden, was metal.

My foot was destroyed and was wedged in the door, only the tough leather sole keeping it open.

My knees gave out and I fell into the doorframe, smacking my head against it.

Then came the sound of gears turning and doors clanking. Through blurred vision, I saw the walls open and the furniture sink inside. The TV and bed both disappeared into the wall.

"Shit!" I cried. "No!"

I realized I sounded like the men on TV. I'd become one of the channels. And I was stuck in the doorframe, the heavy door keeping me in place. I pushed on it, trying to open it, but it wouldn't budge.

Any second now, fire would rain down or steal spikes would shoot from the walls.

"Isabelle, please!" I cried out. "You don't need to do this!"

I knew it was too late. I'd let her get away.

Is she in on this? Or is she a victim too? Did someone take her from the bathroom, or did she escape?

"Please, Isabelle!" I tried once more. "Don't do this to me."

A spout came out of the ceiling over where the bed had once been. Another appeared closer to the bathroom and one further away.

"Oh fuck! No! No! Fuck!"

I was going to die. I knew it. I'd watched two others go and now I'd be on a video too, with Diablo Snuff at the bottom right corner of my screen.

"Let me the fuck out of here!" I tried again.

I lost it. I guess adrenaline took over because, in my fit of rage, I finally started to push the door open. My foot was destroyed but the rest of my body was fueled by anger, fear, and a will to live.

The spout came to life and acid rained down from the ceiling. The scent singed my nose hairs and the sizzling as it hit the floor was like knives through my skull. A drop hit my shoe and fried it. I kicked it off just before it ate its way to my foot.

"No, motherfucker!" I screamed as I shoved my way through the bathroom door and fell onto the floor, clutching my shattered foot. The pain was unbearable. But I was alive. Acid sizzled outside the bathroom door, and through the window at the shower stall, I saw it decimate Isabelle's clothes, her shoes, and my T-shirt and socks.

A second later and it would have melted me where I stood.

6

The urge to call out for help was almost overwhelming, but I realized no one who could hear me would be coming to my aid. They might not even know I'd survived. I was supposed to die out there in that empty room, my body disintegrated by the acid rain, and those motherfuckers had planned for it to happen. My only benefit was in them thinking I was dead.

I forced myself up onto my one good, bare foot, and grabbed the bathroom counter for support.

Where did Isabelle go?

I looked around the bathroom for some kind of back door. There was no trapdoor in the floor, there was no drawstring for an attic escape, so where the hell had she gone? The shower. That's where she'd been. I'd seen her go in there. I'd seen her in the steam as she'd started to wash herself.

Yes, she was in the shower.

I hopped as slowly as possible, trying not to shake my foot too much. Each jerk sent lightning through my body. It hurt so badly.

When I reached the stall, I yanked the door open to find it empty. I wasn't expecting to see her standing there, but I thought there might at least be an escape hatch. Hope was almost lost when I noticed that halfway down the wall there was a white piece of fabric.

I reached out and touched it. A frayed piece of towel. I looked over at the plastic pouch sitting on the counter, the one she must've carried into the bathroom earlier. One towel and the condom remained. She'd taken the other towel, wrapped it around herself, and fucking ditched me.

The bitch left me there to die. I knew she had. I'd known it from the moment I saw the others suffering on the TV. Yet, there'd been a shard of hope, a piece of me that believed it might not be true. An even larger part that thought things might not end the same for me. That maybe Isabelle had accidentally fallen for me.

You're not that charming. You're not that unbelievably great.

Deep down I understood what was going on, at least on the exterior. She'd duped me. Isabelle had strung me along all night and dragged me to this place only to see me suffer.

But why?

What sense would that make?

Who could possibly gain something from this?

Was someone selling these videos?

More importantly, how could someone be so vile? So evil? How could Isabelle wear that mask of sweetness, of instant friendship, of a romantic lover so easily if her true intention was to punish me?

Seeing this shred of evidence, this piece of the towel she'd worn in her escape, infuriated me. I wanted revenge.

Against Isabelle.

Against whomever she worked for.

Against whatever the fuck Diablo Snuff was.

The few seconds I stared through that glass and out into the room full of acid rain was a moment of clarity. It was a thunderstorm meant to peel the flesh from my bones, melt the meat, and disintegrate the rest of me into glops of mushy goo that would run down the slightly declining floor toward the room's center. I touched my own chest and thought of how I could right now be dripping into that drain.

It was time to get out of here. Turning my attention back to the wall, I felt along the tile grout lines, searching for some sort of secret door. My hand pressed against a loose tile and it acted as a button. The entire wall swung open much faster and easier than I expected, coming unstuck with the same sucking sound a refrigerator makes when the door breaks the seal. I fell through it with my arms flailing and stepped hard on my broken foot.

Lightning lit up my insides as I fought with every ounce of strength I had to keep my scream on the inside of my body. Fiery pain leapt up from my foot to my groin and all the way to my throat where I felt bile build up and threaten to spill out.

My shoulder struck the dark, dirty, and damp wall in front of me. I would've fallen over if not for the lantern holder attached to the wall. I grabbed it and hung on as I silently handled my pain, screaming with my mouth closed to stifle the sound. The shower door closed behind me.

I couldn't look at my foot. I knew it was at an awkward angle. Seeing it would only make me throw up, and I was doing everything in my power to fight that urge. I steadied myself against the wall and waited for my eyes to adjust.

The space between the walls of the Love Bug push button was a dark corridor with only the faint glow of lantern lights hung every thirty feet or so to illuminate the black, metal, and rusting walls.

It didn't seem like I was on the other side of hotel rooms but more like I was walking down a boiler room hallway. Strange sounds filled the air, things you'd expect to hear in a nightmare.

Water dripped somewhere in the distance.

Gears shifted.

Locks slammed shut.

A music box played softly from far away.

Strange hissing.

Muffled voices that sounded like people begging from all different directions. Males, females, and a mixture of the two.

Screams. Agonizing screams joined the disharmony of hectic and maddening sound.

This was hell. Or what you'd imagine hell to be like.

Behind me, the hall seemed to go on forever and in front of me was the same. Doors lined one side of the hallway, my left side now, at intervals that I imagined put them at the exact opposite of the garage doors outside. Every room had its backdoor for one maniacal mother-fucker to sneak out and leave their victim ensnared in their trap.

Fill my cunt with your seed!

I blinked and saw her.

Isabelle was riding me, her body and face morphing to that of the black-tarred devil. The demon with the forked tongue.

Fill my cunt with your seed!

What had I done?

I was tempted to yell Isabelle's name. I wanted to find her, to force her to explain, to choke the shit out of her. I'd never laid a hand on a woman, but if ever one deserved some physical abuse, it was the one who'd stolen my seed, fucked me into a trance, and then left me to be disintegrated in a shower of acid rain.

The hallway seemed endless and with my foot a heap of broken bone and cartilage, I dreaded trying to navigate it. I had to hop forward one quiet step at a time, lean against the wall, and drag my bad foot behind me.

As I carefully crept forward, I thought of how I'd met Isabelle earlier that evening. She'd been so beautiful sitting behind me, warning me not to go with the prostitutes. Oh, how I wished I'd just gone with the hookers. Chances were, they would've gone with me to a regular hotel room, not dragged me out to the middle of nowhere to be slaughtered for the camera.

The camera.

Who was on the other end of that thing? Who was watching these repulsive acts? Who was getting off on this?

Diablo Snuff.

The logo at the bottom of the screen kept coming back to me. What the fuck was Diablo Snuff?

Another scream sounded off right behind me. I turned painfully on my heel and nearly ran right into the woman who came charging through the iron door. This one was completely naked, blonde, and nearly as gorgeous as Isabelle. Her hair was wet, her tits red and pocked with bite marks, her pussy unshaven and dripping with shower water.

Another Isabelle.

"You!" I growled.

"Que?" she said. "What... who..."

I grabbed her throat and slammed her up against the wall.

"Who's in there?" I asked.

She tried to shake her head but my hold on her was too tight.

"Let's go see!" I said.

"No."

I grabbed the wheel-like handle on the door and pulled it open. With her hair wrapped around my fist, I held onto her like a crutch as I hopped forward and yanked her into the shower with me. She screamed and smacked at my arm, trying to break free from my grip, but I pulled back hard on her scalp and wrapped my other hand around her throat.

"Quit struggling or I'll break your goddamn neck," I warned. "You have no idea what I've gone..."

My words trailed off as I stared at the scene in front of me. The room was identical to mine. And as I stood in the shower, staring through the glass partition, I watched as three gigantic wolf-like creatures chewed up the man on the other side. Their hair was black, matted with blood, and they tore into the man's body like starving beasts.

One animal ripped at his face while another yanked flesh from his stomach. His entrails were strewn all over the place. The third creature stared at me. Its eyes glowed an odd, milky white like the luster of an iridescent pearl. Saliva dripped and dangled from its mouth in long unbroken strings as it glared at me and growled.

"Sick him!" I heard the bitch next to me yell.

The creature's face twisted into a look of pure hatred and evil. Its snout pulled back to reveal giant teeth.

The dog, or whatever it was, ran, leapt through the air, and crashed through the glass of the shower stall just as I smashed the bitch's head into the door and tossed her out into the hallway. I slammed the door shut just as the demon dog rammed into it on the other side.

Her body hit the floor with a sickening thud. I looked down to see her nose was broken, blood collecting in a pool near her head.

"Fucking cunt," I spat.

I was never a fan of the word, but it suited her properly. The fucking cunt got the man on the other side killed and tried to do the same to me. And she'd just come through the door only seconds before, meaning she must've stayed in the shower long enough to watch the man get attacked. She'd gotten off on it.

I reached down the best I could and slapped her leg, checking to see if she was awake. She wasn't. She was out cold.

"Fuck," I swore under my breath. "There goes my crutch."

I didn't want to leave her there. What if she woke up and charged at me from behind or ran to tell someone I'd survived? Well, she'd been heading right at me when she came out of the door so at least I knew I was going in the right direction. What I was going to do when I reached wherever she'd been headed was a complete mystery.

I had no weapon. I had no plan. I had no idea what I'd be confronting.

The only thing I had was the element of surprise, and I wasn't even sure I still had that. I knew somebody was recording the rooms, but were they being watched live as well? If so, I was fucked. Someone would have seen me escape.

I heard yelling from a couple of doors down.

"Hello!" came the muffled voice.

A door opened and I squatted down quickly, hoping to not be seen. I was lucky. A man ran out, naked and wet, his dick swinging as he cackled and ran away from me and towards the end of the hallway.

Men do this too?

I hobbled over to the door he'd exited and yanked it open. Through the shower window, I saw a woman pulling on her pants. She had long, wavy red hair and pale skin. She wrapped a bra around herself, fastened it, and turned it to cup it over her tits.

She was pretty enough to be one of the evil seductresses. What if I was being tricked again and she was one of the bad ones?

She yelled something but it wasn't English and didn't sound Spanish. Then she followed it with, "Javier, hurry up in there! I need you to take me back to the casino."

The casino. Is that where they all operate? They hang out and wait for assholes like me?

Javier was the man's name. Like Isabelle. This woman wasn't one of the evil ones. She turned to look at the shower and noticed Javier wasn't in it. As I stood in the doorway, watching her through the glass, she noticed me and began to panic.

"Who? What the fuck? Who are you?" she asked in English but with an accent that could have been Russian.

"There's no time!" I yelled. "Get in here. Come to the bathroom."

There was no way I was hopping out to talk to her on the other side.

"Where is Javier?" she asked as she stood up.

The whirring kicked on, the loud crank of the furniture retracting into the walls. She stepped away from the bed, watching in shock as it dragged her shirt with it on its way to the wall. Whatever was planned would be happening in a matter of seconds. I banged an open palm against the shower window to bring her attention back to me. She turned and looked at me, confusion on her face.

"Javier?" she asked again.

"He left you!" I yelled. "Come on! Get in here. Now! You'll die out there!"

She approached slowly, cautiously, just as the mirrored ceiling above her opened up.

"Hurry!" I yelled.

Understandably, she didn't trust me, but she would die because of it if she didn't hurry.

"Please!" I shouted. "You're gonna fucking die out there! Get in here!"

I banged at the window again.

She turned to look up at the ceiling, clearly having no idea the real danger she was in. How would she? She hadn't seen the videos. She only knew she was in a strange, empty room and her lover had disappeared.

Then it happened.

The bathroom door slammed shut, locking her inside the room.

I heard the hissing sound before I saw them.

Snakes.

They fell right where she'd been standing only seconds before, crashing to the ground, a heap of pissed off killers. Multicolored and angry, they writhed around on the ground. She screamed and backed into the window, staring at the evil gift she'd received.

I looked around for something I could use to break the window, but there was nothing. The bathroom was as empty as mine had been, with nothing more than a sink and a bar of soap.

The closest thing to me was the metal towel rack. I smashed a closed fist against it, surprised that it tore free on one side. With all the strength I could muster, I yanked and twisted until the other side broke apart from the wall.

Outside the window, one of the snakes snapped at her. She slid out of the way. She banged on the window with her closed fist, keeping her back to me, watching the serpents dance around her.

These weren't ordinary snakes. They'd done this before. They sensed a victim in their presence without the need to be provoked. They'd been triggered just by dropping through the ceiling.

Another snapped and this one sunk its teeth into her knee. She howled in pain, yanked it loose, and threw it. It snapped at her face as she tossed it in the air. It missed and fell back into the crowd of angry snakes.

"Watch out!" I yelled.

She couldn't move out of the way as the only way for her to go was directly into the pit of beasts.

I held the metal towel bar over my head and slammed it into the window. It cracked but didn't shatter. I didn't have the same kind of power that an angry demon dog had. I pulled back and hit it again and again. With the last strike, it shattered, and the girl fell through the window and into me, knocking me into the wall behind me.

My head slammed into the tile and she stepped on my broken foot. I cried out and grabbed her waist to prevent my fall.

The snakes were coming.

"In here," I yelled as I stumbled through the secret wall.

She followed behind me and crashed to the floor in the corridor. She tried to get up to a crawling position, but her eyes were struggling to remain open. Her mouth was open, and her tongue lolled out.

The snake bite. I'd only seen her get bitten once, but who knew how many had gotten to her before I broke open the window.

"Come on," I said. "Stay with me. What's your name?"

"Vivian," she replied, just barely getting the word out.

"Okay, listen, Vivian. We're gonna get out of here. The two of us. You and me. We're gonna get out of here, okay? But you have to keep your eyes open and you have to stand up long enough to get out of this building. It's not safe where we are. And I can't carry you."

Her head hung down. She couldn't do it. She didn't even have the energy to crawl let alone walk.

Grief overwhelmed me. I'd barged through the door and shattered the glass to help her, but I'd been too late. She'd gotten bitten by the snake anyway. If my foot hadn't been fucked up, I would've reacted quicker.

Her eyes closed.

"Vivian," I said again as I snapped my finger right next to her ear.

She collapsed to the floor and lay there, a heap of flesh, no longer responding to my requests or commands.

"She's dead," thundered an unseen voice. "The venom in her veins has already eaten its way through her body."

It was loud like it was coming from a megaphone or hidden speakers in the wall. The voice was strange and disturbing, garbled. It was deep and then it was soft. It was that of an old man, then a young man, and then a small child.

You've heard something similar. When you were fucking Isabelle. Her voice did that.

"You sick fucks!" I yelled.

Being quiet was no longer important. They, whoever they were, knew I'd survived.

7

I expected a response. Maybe a warning. A threat. Something. Yet, once the voice told me Vivian was dead, it went silent. My element of surprise was gone. They knew I was alive.

Now what?

I checked Vivian once more. The voice was correct. She was gone. Dead.

What could they have gotten from her? Isabelle wanted your seed, but what would they have taken from her? Is it only about the videos? God, help me.

Anger shot through me and adrenaline filled my veins, helping me stand back up and limp down the corridor. I needed to reach the end. Saving people was no longer my priority. I wanted to find the owner of that psychotic voice and rip out his fucking vocal chords.

I reached the end of the hall and found nothing. I'd been expecting to enter some sort of control room or an office. I found none of that. Only a cement wall.

I backed up and stared at it, scanned it for a handle or a button or hinges.

This can't be.

I hopped back to the wall and felt around, thinking maybe I'd push open a new secret door, but I felt only solid concrete. It wouldn't budge.

Where had these evil fucks been headed?

Each had run in this direction. I was defeated. Trapped. I turned around and looked down the hall. Nothing but dim corridor lay before me. I supposed there could have been a back door at the other side of the building, but that was a long way to walk, and I was exhausted, injured, and armed with only a towel rack bar.

This is too insane. This has to be a nightmare.

I remembered waking up that morning and having breakfast with my buddies in the hotel. It was all fried food. Fried dough, tortillas, eggs, and bacon.

I remembered lounging by the pool for a couple of hours sipping mojitos. The waitress was pretty, and we joked about how my drinks seemed a lot stronger than my buddies'.

I remembered having diarrhea shortly after, probably from the sushi at the bar.

I remembered being at the casino that night and sitting at the same table as my friend Pete as he got a hand job underneath the table from a prostitute, the same one he'd taken upstairs.

I remembered sitting at the burger joint with Isabelle.

Of course, I remembered her naked body all over me and the way I slammed her against the wall and drove into her.

This can't be a nightmare, right?

I wanted to collapse on the floor and give up. But then I saw the door, the closest one to the end of the hallway. It looked like all the other iron doors I'd passed. Like all the others that led to shower stalls.

What if this last one is the way out?

Barging into the room could lead me into a trap, so I approached slowly and pressed my forehead against it for a second, listening to see if I could hear anyone being tortured inside or the sound of someone showering. All was silent.

I opened the door and stepped into the shower.

The bathroom was dark. The stall was dry. Through the glass window, I saw the TV was on, but the channel was set to static. The white flicker cast an eerie glow over the empty room. The bed was in place as well as all the other furniture.

Poltergeist taught me that staticky TVs could never be trusted. This was a setup. If I walked out into that room, I'd be met with the most horrifying death yet.

What could be worse than fire, metal stakes, acid rain, demon dogs, or venomous snakes?

Yet, I felt compelled to enter the room, like my escape waited in there. It wasn't like I had any other choice. My only other option was to head back in the direction from which I came and see if there was a backdoor. There wouldn't be one. In fact, I thought, there might not be an escape at all.

The glow in the room changed from the flickering white to multi-colored hues. Then I heard it. The sound of two people having wild, hot sex. The woman was moaning, and the man was grunting.

Then I heard a familiar voice say, "I'm a pussy?"

It was a video of Isabelle and me.

I didn't feel myself doing it, but I unknowingly made my way out of the bathroom and into the bedroom. I sat down at the foot of the bed and stared up at the TV screen where Isabelle was there, naked in all her glory, riding me.

I snapped out of it and realized I'd put myself in a terrible position. Before I had the chance to get out of there, I heard the gears shift and the bathroom door slam shut.

What the hell were you thinking?

The TV had put me in a trance-like state. I didn't even realize I'd drifted toward it, and now I was trapped in the final room of that hallway.

"No!" I yelled.

The furniture and TV remained but the mirrored ceiling opened. I threw my hands to my face, a lame attempt at protecting myself from whatever may come, and I backed away from the bed.

But nothing dropped out of the gaping hole. I stared up into the black box above the bed and saw them. Figures stared down at me. Each wore a hood over his or her head, leaving their faces shrouded in darkness. I couldn't make out any features. There must have been ten of them watching me.

One of them lowered a metal ladder and backed away. As if on cue, they all turned and moved away from the hole, disappearing into the darkness and leaving me alone in the room with only my personal porn video and the ladder that could either be my escape or a slow climb to my death.

What other choice do you have?

I climbed onto the bed and made my way to the ladder. I had no other option. This was it. I gripped the railings and hopped one rung at a time on my good foot, struggling to keep my metal towel rack bar in my hand. As I leaned forward, the metal felt cold against my bare chest. When I reached the top, I poked my head up first but saw only darkness. So, I climbed the rest of the way out of the hole.

Someone pulled up the ladder and then the hole sealed shut behind me, leaving me standing in a pitch-black void. I held my fists up in front of my face, my metal bar raised like a baseball bat, ready to fight if I needed to, and it was so dark I couldn't see a thing. All was silent. A cold chill hit me, and it stunk like raw sewage.

My fingers instinctively shot to my nose, but before I could squeeze my nostrils shut, the awful stench was replaced by a floral one, like roses and jasmine. It was soft and pleasant, but I got the sense it was meant to cover the first foul odor, the same way one might spray an air freshener after taking a horrendous shit.

"You're here," a soft, sweet voice said.

"Isabelle?" I asked.

It was strange hearing her voice but not seeing her face. I wondered how many others were in the room with us.

"I knew you could do it," she said.

"Bullshit, you tried to have me killed."

"No, baby. We tested you. It's what we do."

"You tested me?" I chuckled.

Light popped on overhead, a strange purplish bulb. And I saw her in front of me. She was dressed in a slick, black, skin-tight vinyl suit and her hair was pulled back in a ponytail. Long streaks of black mascara jutted out from the corners of her eyes and her lips were painted in deep crimson. It was a uniform of some sort. She looked stunning, like she was about to take the stage in an erotic play. Even after what she'd done to me, I was drawn to her, and I couldn't figure out why.

She's done something to you. She's poisoned your mind.

"Who's we?" I asked. "As in *we* tested you?"

Then I saw them lined up behind her, no less than twenty figures, all wearing strange black masks. Some wore bird masks while others wore goats. The purple light seeped between them and only highlighted bits and pieces, keeping them in an ominous shadow at all times.

"We are *we*," she replied.

This was the point of no return. I wasn't foolish enough to believe I'd get out of here alive. Trying to remain calm and be cordial would get me nowhere. This was that point where all hope was lost, and I might as well say what was on my mind.

"Murderers!" I yelled. "You killed that guy with the dogs, and you killed Vivian with the snakes, and you tried to kill me with acid. You sick fucks!"

"I understand your anger," Isabelle said calmly.

She was too relaxed. If she'd spit on me and cursed me or screamed reasons why an American tourist deserved to die, at least I would have an excuse for her actions. At least I would know she believed in something that led her to make the decisions she'd made, but instead, she gave me a soft, pleasant voice with absolutely no fucking meaning behind it.

The worst part was she looked so good delivering her tranquil non-explanation. Even with rage running through my veins, I wanted to grab her and pull her tight against my body.

"I understand," Isabelle repeated and took a step closer.

She understands you, Michael. She really understands you.

It wasn't my own voice in my head. How was this possible? What the fuck was she doing to me?

She understands you. Trust her.

"Come here, baby," Isabelle said. She held her hands out as if wanting a hug. And I wanted to hug her. I wanted to be in her arms. Was it something in the air? Some sort of spell? Was she a witch?

"No," I whispered, finding it so hard to deny her.

I sensed the others in the room. I could see them behind her, slightly out of focus, but it didn't matter. Only Isabelle mattered.

"You want me again?" she asked as she pulled the top of her vinyl suit down, revealing her beautiful naked tits.

I wanted to take them in my mouth, and I didn't care that others were in the room.

"Do you know why you want me right now?" she asked.

I didn't.

"Because you're just like us. You're a sexually charged murderer."

"No, I'm not," I argued.

"You are, Michael," she said. "Do you remember what you did to Stan?"

Stan? Stan who?

"Stanley Mitchell, Michael. Do you remember?"

Stanley Mitchell?

Rebecca, in the office, came to me and told me how Stanley had been leaving her love letters. She showed them to me. One after another, they got increasingly more sexually suggestive. Then he cornered her in the parking lot and insisted she was leading him on. That he only wanted to go on a date with her. He tried to drag her to his car, but she fought him off. I had no choice but to fire him when I saw the security camera footage. Rebecca even took out a restraining order.

"I fired Stanley Mitchell because he was a sick son of a bitch," I said barely above a whisper, my eyes on Isabelle's naked upper body.

"That's not true, Michael," Isabelle said. "You fired him because you wanted to fuck Rebecca again, and you were angry that he was stepping in on your territory."

She's right. You wanted to fuck Rebecca again. One drunken post-holiday party hookup wasn't enough. You were angry that Stanley was harassing her because you wanted her.

The voice in my head wasn't mine. It wasn't true. Yes, I'd fucked

Rebecca once, but we'd both agreed it was a mistake.

"You are as sexually charged as I am," Isabelle said as she crept closer and put her hands on my shoulders. Her fingers touched the tender spot where she'd taken a bite out of me, and as she did, my knees wobbled. The pressure against my shoulder made my cock stir. It was a sweet pain that felt so good but hurt so bad at the same time.

"He was a sick fuck, and I fired him," I repeated.

"Did you know he hanged himself three months later?" Isabelle asked.

I hadn't heard that.

"He did?" I said aloud.

"He did," Isabelle assured me. "You killed him, Michael. It was your fault. You wanted so badly to fuck Rebecca again, and that made you hate Stanley so much. You told him he was a disgusting human being, that you'd make sure he never worked again, and that he needed to seek help. He was jobless and depressed for three months. Now, he's dead."

"I didn't kill him," I argued. "His decision was his decision. That has nothing to do with me."

"You're a murderer, Michael," Isabelle said as she reached down and cupped her hand around my cock. "Join us and do what you were born to do. Do you know how many people get off on watching our videos? You can be a part of that. You can be a part of something bigger."

"No. I'm not like you."

"Of course not," Isabelle said as she looked back at the crowd behind her. Some of the masked murderers shrugged and some giggled. "You know why else you're so attracted to me, Michael?" she asked as she unzipped me and wrapped her warm hand around my cock. "We're one now. We're connected. You've given me your seed. I'm going to give birth to your child soon. Our numbers will grow by one, and he will have your strength and tenacity. He'll have my beauty and hatred for the world. If you become one of us, we can be a family."

What a sick fucking family that would be.

I shook my head.

"You only have to accept that you're like us," she added. "Drop to your knees and give your soul."

I shook my head again.

"What good is a soul anyway?" she asked. "You don't use yours. Besides, you want to hurt people. I felt it when you were fucking me. You want to fuck me and hurt me now."

"No," I whispered.

But as I looked down, I realized I'd dropped my pants and my cock was rock hard. I didn't remember pulling them down. Had she removed them? When I looked up again, Isabelle was bent over in front of me. She'd peeled off the rest of her suit and was leaning forward, her pussy lips swollen at the tip of my cock, just begging to be fucked.

I couldn't. I didn't want to.

But you do want to. So bad. You want to fill her with your seed again. You want to stuff her and fill her until you're pouring out from between her folds and running down her legs. You want to be a part of her family, and the only way to do that is to give her that seed.

Moans filled the room. I looked past Isabelle to see that the other masked figures were engaged in a giant orgy. They'd all thrown off their robes and were naked except the strange masks still strapped to their faces.

One man with a gigantic cock fucked a woman doggy style in front of me. His dick looked beastly, too large to be real. And she took it all in, screaming in agony but laughing with joy at the same time.

A sexy redhead rode a guy, hopping up and down on him and giggling hysterically.

One woman growled with what sounded like demonic rage as another woman ate her out.

And then I felt her. Isabelle's pussy smothered my cock, wrapping around it, soaking me with her juices as she backed into me, not giving me the opportunity to protest. I dropped my metal bar to the ground with a clang and reached for her hips.

"Yes!" she yelled.

Her insides massaged me like before and I knew this was the place

I wanted to be. To be with Isabelle forever would be my version of heaven.

I gripped her hips and pounded her, driving into her with as much force as my damaged foot would allow.

In fact, as I slid into her and back out, I realized each thrust seemed to be healing my foot. I was able to put my full weight on it now. It ached, but less and less as I continued to fuck her.

New lights flickered on around us, different colors, like they came from a disco ball. I realized we were surrounded by counters with screens, like we were in some sort of air traffic control room. So many images flashed around me.

And I was smiling.

"Oh, yes!" Isabelle cried out as she backed into me.

Hundreds of these screens surrounded us. I glanced at each one, never fully taking my attention off the woman in front of me. On screen after screen I saw people having sex. In so many positions, with so many toys, involving so many strange situations.

But not all the screens showed sexual pleasures. Many displayed people screaming in agony. One man's skin was flayed from his body. Another was bent over while a wooden rod was shoved up his ass. The images got worse and worse, and I couldn't stop fucking Isabelle.

My desire for her was stronger than my hatred of these videos with the Diablo Snuff logo at the bottom right of each screen.

"We will be a family!" Isabelle yelled as she looked over her shoulder at me.

It felt even better than before. Her pussy was getting warmer and warmer, hotter and hotter, and I throbbed inside her.

"Fuck me!" she yelled.

"Fuck me," came a man's voice.

I looked to the right to see a man bent over just like Isabelle while a masked man fucked him in the ass.

"Fuck me!" a woman yelled.

I looked to my left to see a woman wearing a strap-on and fucking a woman doggy style who was bent over one of the video control panels.

"Fuck me!" Isabelle said again.

I reached around, grabbed her right tit, and pinched her nipple hard as I drove into her.

"Be one of us and you can fuck me like this forever," Isabelle said. "Do you want that?"

"I do," I whispered.

I suddenly got lightheaded and I fell backward onto the floor, my bare ass hitting the tile.

"What's wrong with you?" she asked. "Don't you want me?"

She didn't give me the chance to answer as she straddled me and sunk down onto my cock. She grinded her hips and closed her eyes, tilting her head back to the sky.

"You want to know what this place is?" came the odd voice I'd heard earlier in the corridor.

A man stepped into view, sliding out of the darkness, dressed in a black suit. He wore a black shirt and tie. He too wore a mask, only his was red and had a long, pointed nose. It was similar to the bird masks but looked more... evil.

Seeing him should have ended my arousal but it didn't. I pinched both of Isabelle's tits and lifted up to fuck her harder.

"This is Diablo Snuff," the man said.

"What... is... this... place?" I asked, fucking her harder with each syllable.

"You see the videos all around you?" he asked. "Who do you think watches these sexual videos ending in death?"

"You," I said.

"Ha," he snickered. "Yes, I do. But not just me, Michael. Terrorists and killers and every other sick individual on the planet. We feed the hunger of the heathens, fill the needs of the ne'er-do-wells, and deliver the devil's delights to the deranged. We fuel evil's fire, Michael. And we're kind of exclusive. Not everyone gets an invitation."

"Be one of us, baby," Isabelle said as she reached back to squeeze my balls. "You can do it. You survived. You're a survivor, just like me."

She rocked on my cock with her fist clenching my balls. It hurt as she squeezed them too tightly, but it felt good at the same time. The pain was intense but felt so fucking incredible.

"You survived?" I asked. "You were brought here like me?"

"Yes," she said. "By Juan Diego."

A big guy, Latino looking, stepped over to us, naked, except for his goat mask. His cock hung in front of Isabelle's face. She reached out, grabbed his dick like it had no feeling, and yanked him closer. She took him in her mouth, stroking him as she sucked him.

It should have disgusted me, but it didn't. I slapped her ass and flipped her over, yanking her mouth off of him as I slammed her on her back.

"You see?" she squealed. "He's one of us!"

"He's one of us!" someone else yelled.

"Be one of us!" another voice called out.

I pressed my body against Isabelle's, loving the feel of my flesh against hers, and gripped her shoulders as I viciously fucked her.

"Give me your seed again, baby," she whispered in my ear. "We'll make some beautiful, evil little monsters to take over this world."

"Fuck and be merry," the man in the suit said. "And bring me more bodies to put in these videos. Just meet young ladies... or men... whatever your preference. We don't discriminate here. Fuck them, enjoy them, and then leave them so we can do the rest."

"You mean kill them?" I asked as I bit Isabelle's nipple and kept fucking her.

"Yes," the man said. "Think of it as a job... more of a lifestyle actually. All the food and drink and drugs and sex one could ever imagine."

"Give me that glorious seed," Isabelle whispered. "Our demons will rule this world. Be one of us. Kill with me, baby. We can have threesomes and kill. I'll be yours forever. Kill with me."

I gripped Isabelle's hair in my fist and squeezed tight as I stuffed her with my cock.

"This will be glorious," the man in the suit sang.

"It will be beautiful," Isabelle said through a deep moan.

Then, as I shoved myself inside of her, each pump suddenly

brought a memory with it.

My foot getting crushed in the door.

"We can fix your foot," the man in the suit said, clearly reading my mind.

The acid rain falling all around me.

"But none of it touched you," he said.

The man getting eaten by the demon dogs.

"You wouldn't have liked him anyway. He was a fucking asshole if truth be told."

Vivian crumpled up on the corridor floor, dead.

"Now that one, yeah that was a fine piece of ass, but she didn't have what it takes to make it here. Not like you. You're special, Michael. You can be part of the program. You can be part of Diablo Snuff."

No, this is wrong.

I wasn't an extremely religious man by no means, but I knew this was wrong. There was good and there was evil. This was definitely evil.

"Yes, we are evil," the man said. "We are all evil, are we not?"

I looked up to see he was holding his hands out, palms up as if waiting for the roar of the crowd. He got it. Different voices all sounded off.

"Evil as fuck!"

"Evil motherfuckers!"

"Tools of the devil!"

"Instruments of evil!"

"Diablo Snuff!"

"This is only the first phase, Michael," the man in the suit said. "We are everywhere. The Dark Master has so many plans for us. Diablo Snuff is everywhere, we are global, universal, and we will end it all. Sign the pact now and you'll live on forever... in ecstasy just like you are right now."

As if handed down to me through a divine power, I remembered Isabelle's words when she first asked my name.

Michael.

"I like that name," she'd said. "It's like the archangel. The one who will lead God's army against the forces of evil."

Everything became clear. The fog inside my mind lifted. That strange voice in my head telling me this was right was gone.

The demon inside Isabelle revealed itself once again. She laughed as she looked in my face, having no idea what I saw. Her eyeballs were pitch black and her mouth hung open in ecstasy. She moaned and grunted as I was still deep inside her, but I'd stopped moving. She was doing the fucking now, and she seemed to notice my lack of movement.

"What is it?" she asked. "Don't you like me anymore?"

She looked into my face with those lifeless eyes, and I knew in her Isabelle form she would break my heart, but it wouldn't work as the demon I saw in her now. She wasn't sweet. She wasn't the angel that tricked me back at the burger joint. She was the monster who'd ridden me in the room, the one who'd cut me, the one who'd left me for dead. Her tongue slithered out and was forked. It lashed at my lip, and even with that disgusting, melted, charred face, her voice came out sweet, "Be with me, Michael. Give me your seed and we'll do this together... forever."

"No," I said quietly.

"Oh yes!" her voice came out deep, in a monstrous growl.

"No, this is wrong."

"Fuck that, it's so right!" she cried out, back in her regular Isabelle state but with eyes still as black as night.

She bucked her hips, trying to force me deeper inside her.

I looked around me and saw everyone fucking. The man in the suit was watching it all with hands clasped in front of him. He had front row seats, the best tickets, to see the greatest orgy the town had to offer. He turned his head from side to side, taking it all in.

Then I saw the window. It was so dark I'd missed it. But the elevated train, perhaps the first one of the morning, drove by just in time for me to see the lights through the glass. We were on the second floor, the office space I'd seen when we first approached the *push button*. This was that large black window.

It's your way out!

I pulled out of Isabelle and her eyes went wide, returning to their original color.

"Michael!" she yelled.

"Evil bitch," I said as I reached out, yanked the mask off of the guy being fucked in the ass to my right, and shoved the sharp nose into her neck. "My seed won't do *shit* for you now!"

I heard her gurgle blood. The moment I pulled my cock out of her, the immense pain returned to my foot. I stood, pulled up my pants, picked up the metal towel rack bar from the floor, and hobbled toward the window with every ounce of strength I had left. A few of the naked demons tried to stop me.

I stabbed one in the eye with the mask. He howled in pain and knocked over some of the other demons. Another leapt at me, claws out, but I swung the metal bar and caught her across the chin with it. She skidded across the ground.

"Where do you think you're going, Michael?" the man in the suit asked.

I was only about five feet from the window when I launched myself at it, remembering the ferocity of the demon dog crashing through the shower wall. I rolled and slammed my shoulder into the glass. It gave way. The window shattered as I flew through it.

"Come back here!" I heard the man in the suit scream.

But I was already tumbling toward the ground. Without much time to steady myself, I was mid-turn when my body smacked against the pavement. My shoulder and thigh took the brunt of the force, and my arm cushioned my head, so it didn't bounce off the cement.

It took me a moment to fight through the wave of pain and another to battle the disbelief of what I'd just gone through. I might've lain there much longer if I didn't fear the Diablo Snuff henchmen racing out onto the street to drag my ass back into the building. They could have, easily. I wouldn't be able to put up much of a fight in my current state.

Outside, the sun was up and had painted the morning a soft orange. Two men standing outside the auto repair shop stared at me as I lay on my stomach, cheek against the street. Each held a tire in his hand. Neither man budged, but they whispered back and forth, probably wondering what the half-naked gringo was doing lying in the middle of the street and why he'd just flown through a window.

Beyond them, the woman who ran the little food shack also watched. She leaned through her pick-up window. Smoke billowed out from whatever she had cooking inside.

Two teenage girls in plaid skirts and polos, on their way to school, had paused and were staring at me, mouths agape. One of the men at the auto shop yelled something at them and the girls walked away, continuing to look over their shoulders at me as they went on their way.

A young man on a bicycle skidded to a halt and was peering up at the building. He had a jug of soapy water dangling from the handlebars of his bike and a squeegee over one shoulder. He, too, was about to start his day's work washing car windows in traffic.

The Panama day had begun while I'd been trapped in a dark hell.

I rolled over and looked up at the window to see the man in the suit, his red mask lifted up to his forehead, displaying a grotesque face that was beyond imagination. His skin was seared and was flaking. His eyes burned a bright yellow.

"Diablo Snuff is everywhere!" he yelled.

"Michael!" I heard Isabelle scream in agony.

"Fuck you," I said. "And fuck Diablo Snuff!"

"This isn't over for you, my friend," the man in the suit warned as he stared down at me. He seemed to realize others in the area were watching. He lowered his mask and glanced at the two men, the woman, the schoolgirls, and the teenage boy.

"People will find out about you," I promised. "You're done."

The hiss of a garbage truck at the end of the street caused me to flinch. For a second, I thought the man in the mask had sent his demons out to get me, but I knew they wouldn't expose themselves any more than they already had. They'd been discovered hiding out in this dark alley.

The man in the mask laughed and said, "You are afraid. Good. You should be." He clapped his hands together softly, and I knew he was applauding me on my escape. *This* escape. There would come a time when I would face Diablo Snuff again, and that time I might not be so lucky.

He clapped once more and in a single flash of light, the entire building folded in on itself. And it was gone. The Love Bug *push button* no longer existed, and in its wake was nothing more than a single gust of wind that blew a piece of newspaper and sent an aluminum beer can tumbling into the street.

All that remained was an empty lot.

The people around me whispered in Spanish. They'd have a story to tell their family members and friends, but at least they'd be safe. Diablo Snuff, whatever it was, had moved on.

I picked myself up and limped down the street towards the train. Somehow, I knew I wouldn't be followed. They wouldn't come after me. At least not today. They'd lost. I'd won.

I knew it wasn't over. Diablo Snuff was only a small part of evil's plan and evil was worldwide. I had my work cut out for me.

That was the first time I encountered true evil. But it wasn't the last.

The end of this story.

Make sure you grab a copy of *The Grindhouse: Diablo Snuff 2* and then read *Passion & Pain: A Diablo Snuff Side Story*. Keep your eyes open for *Slaughter Box: A Diablo Snuff Side Story* and *The Maddening: Diablo Snuff 3*. They'll be out soon and may already be out by the time you read this book.

Stay tuned for the next Carver Pike horror or dark fantasy.

Thanks for reading!

Carver Pike

Oh and if you liked this book, please review it on your favorite sites. Reviews mean so much in this game and every single one helps. Thanks again.

ABOUT THE AUTHOR

My name is Carver Pike. Since as far back as I can remember, I've been fascinated by everything horror. I'd sit cross-legged in front of the TV and watch The Texas Chainsaw Massacre while devouring a bowl of Kaboom cereal. I always wished the ghost at the end of each episode of Scooby-Doo wouldn't be just another man behind the mask. I wanted real ghastly ghouls, dastardly demons, and malevolent monsters.

At some point, I knew I couldn't sit back and keep watching this horror world from the stands. I wanted to be in the game. So, now I wield this virtual pen and sling ink onto this page with the hopes of someday being a major player. I want to create those worlds you visit, feed that fear that keeps you up late at night, and entertain you in ways only the greatest storytellers can.

I'm currently living in Central America with my wife and four kids. When I'm not writing, you can find me watching horror movies with my family or interacting with readers on social media.

Hopefully, we'll form a great author-reader relationship and you'll come to trust that Carver Pike will always keep you entertained.

Check out http://www.CarverPike.com for more info.

ALSO BY CARVER PIKE

The Edge of Reflection Series

Twisted Mirrors

Figments of Fear

Seed of Sin

The Fractured Fallen

Diablo Snuff Series

A Foreign Evil

Passion & Pain: A Diablo Snuff Side Story

The Grindhouse

Grad Night

Redgrave

Shadow Puppets: Scarecrows of Minnow Ranch

The Collective Series (a 10-episode multi-author series)

We All Fall Down: Quills and Daggers 2 (Episode 10)